DEATH MASK!

Moving soundlessly, Nancy peered into the hallway. She heard muffled footsteps, as if someone was walking around the apartment.

But who? And how did the intruder get in?

Nancy sneaked toward the living room. Halfway down the hall a floorboard creaked under her foot. She paused and held her breath. The noise from the other room stopped. The person had heard her!

Nancy rushed into the living room. A figure wearing a ski mask and dressed in black was slipping through the closed curtains and out the sliding glass door.

"Stop!" Nancy hollered. She raced across the carpet and pushed through the curtains covering the door. As she stepped onto the narrow balcony, someone grabbed her arm and flung her toward the railing.

Nancy screamed. She was going to fly off the balcony!

Nancy Drew & Hardy Boys SuperMysteries

DOUBLE CROSSING
A CRIME FOR CHRISTMAS
SHOCK WAVES
DANGEROUS GAMES
THE LAST RESORT
THE PARIS CONNECTION
BURIED IN TIME
MYSTERY TRAIN
BEST OF ENEMIES
HIGH SURVIVAL
NEW YEAR'S EVIL
TOUR OF DANGER
SPIES AND LIES
TROPIC OF FEAR
COURTING DISASTER
HITS AND MISSES
EVIL IN AMSTERDAM
DESPERATE MEASURES
PASSPORT TO DANGER
HOLLYWOOD HORROR
COPPER CANYON CONSPIRACY
DANGER DOWN UNDER
DEAD ON ARRIVAL

Available from ARCHWAY Paperbacks

DEAD ON ARRIVAL

Carolyn Keene

AN ARCHWAY PAPERBACK
Published by POCKET BOOKS
New York London Toronto Sydney Tokyo Singapore

This book is a work of fiction. Names, characters, places and incidents are products of the author's imagination or are used fictitiously. Any resemblance to actual events or locales or persons, living or dead, is entirely coincidental.

AN ARCHWAY PAPERBACK *Original*

An Archway Paperback published by
POCKET BOOKS, a division of Simon & Schuster Inc.
1230 Avenue of the Americas, New York, NY 10020

Produced by Mega-Books, Inc.

ISBN: 0-671-88461-1

First Archway Paperback printing May 1995

10 9 8 7 6 5 4 3 2 1

Cover art by Brian Kotzky

Printed in the U.S.A.

IL 6+

DEAD ON ARRIVAL

Chapter One

"FINALLY, an evening all to ourselves," Nancy Drew said to her boyfriend, Ned Nickerson.

"Only because Bess and George are on vacation with their parents," Ned said teasingly.

"That's not true, Ned, and you know it," Nancy said with mock indignation. "I don't spend all my time with them."

"Not *all,*" Ned agreed. "The rest of the time you're chasing halfway around the world on one case or another."

Nancy had to laugh. "I think you're exaggerating, Ned." Smiling, she reached across the table and took his hand in hers. Reflected candlelight flickered in his brown eyes. He was wearing a light brown sports jacket and a pale yellow button-down shirt. A lock of his thick, brown hair curled softly on his forehead. Nancy thought he was the cutest guy at the restaurant—and in all of River Heights.

"Still," Nancy went on, "it *has* been a long time since we had a night to ourselves. Too long."

"You look beautiful," Ned said in a low voice, leaning forward in his chair.

"Thanks," Nancy smiled. She had hoped Ned would notice. She'd chosen the blue knit dress carefully, knowing that it accentuated her blue eyes and slim figure.

"I'm glad I've got a whole week for spring break," Ned said. Leaning back, he picked up his knife and spread some butter on a piece of hot, freshly baked bread. The Riverside Restaurant was famous for its great food, but Nancy had chosen it for its romantic atmosphere as well.

"That means we can have a whole week of wonderful evenings together," Nancy said.

Ned snorted. "Yeah, with Frank and Joe Hardy," he said. "Nancy, how long are they staying at your house?"

Nancy shot Ned a teasing grin. "Why? Are you jealous?"

Ned pretended to be shocked. "Me? Jealous? Just because two good-looking detectives are staying at your house while your dad's out of town? No way!"

"Well, you don't have anything to worry about," Nancy reassured him. "Frank and Joe are spending all their time on a case for Chief McGinnis. They're working undercover as emergency medical technicians for the River Heights Rescue Squad. They're on the night shift, which means they'll be gone from six P.M. to six A.M., so I'll never even see them. Besides, Hannah's there."

"Just out of curiosity—why did McGinnis pick the Hardys to work on this case instead of two police detectives?" Ned asked.

"The rescue squad works closely with the police department, which means they'd recognize any officer McGinnis put undercover." Nancy reached for a breadstick. "I knew Joe and Frank were taking emergency medical care training as an elective in high school, so I suggested to Chief McGinnis that he talk to them."

Ned shrugged. "I guess it makes sense. They *could* have stayed at a motel, though."

Nancy put down her bread stick and reached for Ned's hand again. "Frank, Joe, and I are friends, okay?" she said softly.

Ned nodded, his grin playful. "Okay." He interlaced his fingers with hers.

This is so nice, Nancy thought. Just the two of us.

"Nancy! I'm so glad I found you," a loud voice rang out across the restaurant, shattering the romantic mood. Nancy twirled in her seat.

A girl her age was striding across the softly lit room, her unbuttoned raincoat flapping against several patrons' chairs.

"Oh, no! It's Brenda Carlton," Nancy whispered to Ned. "What do you think she wants?"

Brenda was a reporter for *Today's Times,* one of River Heights's daily newspapers. Brenda fancied herself an ace crime reporter and thought nothing of sticking her nose into Nancy's investigations.

Ned groaned and rolled his eyes. "Who knows what she wants. But let's hope it doesn't take long. I want to enjoy my dinner—not listen to her boast about what a great reporter she is."

"Nancy. Ned. Hello," Brenda said. She grabbed a chair, pulled it up to their table, and turned toward Nancy. "Have I got a great case for you."

Nancy's brows shot up. "*You're* giving me a case?"

"Sure, why not?" With a nonchalant shrug, Brenda reached for a slice of bread and the dish of butter. "We've worked together before."

"Oh? That was working together?" Nancy replied calmly. "I thought you were just trying to show me up."

"And this is such a juicy case, you won't want to miss it," Brenda said as if she hadn't heard Nancy.

Just then the waiter came up, holding a tray. "Crab cakes for the lady and gentleman," he said as he placed plates in front of Nancy and Ned.

"Could I have hot tea?" Brenda asked the waiter. "Lemon—no sugar, and maybe another basket of bread and extra . . ."

As Brenda rattled on, Ned gave Nancy a pained look. Nancy merely shrugged. She could hardly tell Brenda to get lost—even though she would have loved to.

When the waiter left, Brenda turned back to Nancy. "So, do you want to hear about it?"

Only if it will get rid of you, Nancy wanted to say. "Sure. If you don't mind our eating while you talk." She took a bite of a crab cake.

"Nope." Brenda reached across Ned's plate to grab another hunk of bread. For a second she was quiet, and Nancy had a chance to observe her. She noticed that the collar of Brenda's white blouse was sticking up.

That's strange, Nancy thought. Brenda usually looks as put together as a store mannequin. And though the reporter was always brusque and bossy, Nancy noticed something different—worry lines between Brenda's brows.

"Do you know who Pam Harter is?" Brenda asked, looking from Nancy to Ned.

Ned nodded. "Sure. She's one of the reporters for your dad's newspaper."

"Right. I think she's his best reporter," Brenda said. "She's always getting great scoops. Well, I've been kind of tagging along with Pam, trying to learn how to be a better reporter."

Amazing, Nancy thought. Brenda was actually admitting she needed to learn something. That was a switch.

"So, is Pam working on something hot?" Ned asked. "Maybe a crime that needs solving by Nancy Drew, River Heights's most famous detective?" he added, winking at Nancy.

Nancy hid a laugh behind her napkin, knowing how much Brenda hated to hear about her accomplishments.

But Brenda didn't even look up. "Yes, Pam is investigating something big, but that's not the problem," she replied. She paused dramatically, then turned to Nancy. "The problem is—Pam's missing."

"Missing?" Nancy repeated. "Are you sure she's not just hot on a lead and doesn't want to be in touch?"

"Positive," Brenda declared. "I was supposed to have lunch with her today, and she never showed up."

"Gee, I wonder why," Ned murmured, and Nancy kicked him under the table.

"I called the *Times* and her apartment, and she's not at either place," Brenda rushed on. "But that's not the only reason I'm worried. Pam *is* working on a really big story—so big she says it will win her a Pulitzer Prize. I don't know what it is, though. She's even kept it a secret from me."

"So you think her missing your lunch date might have to do with her story?" Nancy asked.

Brenda nodded. "But that's not all. She's also dating Blaine Young, this big deal architect in Chicago, and their relationship is really volatile. One minute they're madly in love, the next minute she hates him. I called his home, and all I got was his answering machine."

"So you think Blaine killed Pam and hid her in

the closet of one of his new buildings?" Ned asked with a straight face.

Nancy bit her lip, trying to keep from laughing. Okay, so Brenda's story was off-the-wall. Still, she seemed genuinely upset. And Nancy *was* kind of curious. She'd always admired Pam Harter's straight-shooting style, and more than once the reporter had angered some River Heights big shot by exposing him or her. Maybe Brenda did have reason to be worried.

"I could investigate this myself," Brenda said, returning to her usual snobby tone, "but I'm working on a big story for Monday's edition and don't have much time."

"So what exactly did you want me to do?" Nancy asked as she took another bite of crab.

Brenda glanced down at her lap. "I thought you could go with me tonight to check out her apartment. You know, make sure everything's all right. I'd do it alone," she added brusquely, "Only I, um—"

"Only you're nervous about going into a dark, spooky apartment all by yourself?" Ned suggested.

Brenda shot him an annoyed look. "Not at all. I just thought Nancy would like to be in on the action."

Sure, Nancy thought. Ned's reason made more sense. Brenda did look nervous.

"Of course if Pam has really disappeared, I get the story first," Brenda added. Raising one hand, she waved it in an arc. "'Missing Reporter Found,' by Brenda Carlton. Has a nice ring to it, don't you think?"

Nancy rolled her eyes. So Brenda did have another motive. She'd get Nancy to do all the detective work, and she'd get the byline.

"Sorry, Brenda, we're busy later," Ned said.

Ignoring him, Brenda directed her gaze at Nancy. "I *am* worried," she said sincerely.

Nancy sighed and put down her fork. "All right. I am kind of curious. But while we're finishing dinner, you'd better call the police and report that she's missing—just in case."

Brenda nodded and, grabbing her shoulder bag, she rose from the chair and headed toward the pay phone.

"What happened to our romantic evening?" Ned asked.

Nancy smiled apologetically. "She's already ruined it. Besides, Brenda may have reason for concern. Pam Harter has written some big exposés."

"Nancy, Pam only stood Brenda up for lunch. It's not as if Brenda received a ransom note," Ned said, tossing down his napkin.

Nancy had to laugh at his disgruntled expression. "Come on, aren't you the least bit curious?"

"No," Ned stated emphatically, but then he grinned. "Okay, so nosing around some gorgeous reporter's apartment might be kind of fun."

Nancy raised one brow. "Who said Pam Harter was gorgeous?"

"I've seen her picture in the *Times.* So come on and eat, Nancy," Ned added with a laugh. "We have a mystery to solve."

"Thanks for letting us into Pam's apartment," Brenda said to Mr. Zeleski, the superintendent of Pam's building. Ned, Nancy, and Brenda were standing on the landing in front of the door marked 3B. Pam lived in a new town house complex in River Heights.

"No problem, Ms. Carlton," Mr. Zeleski said as he pushed open the door. "I know you two are friends."

"So, you haven't seen Ms. Harter at all today, Mr. Zeleski?" Nancy asked as Ned and Brenda entered the apartment.

He shook his head. "But I live in the end unit, so I don't see everything that goes on."

"Thanks," Nancy said as she stepped inside the apartment. Ned and Brenda were standing in the small foyer.

"Pam? Are you here?" Brenda called nervously.

"Why don't we spread out and look around?" Nancy suggested.

"Uh, I think I'll stay with you," Brenda said.

Nancy walked slowly into the living room–dining room combo, Brenda tagging on her heels. The area was tastefully decorated in gray with pastel accents. Except for books and magazines scattered around, the room was neat. Curtains were closed over a sliding glass door. When

Nancy pushed them back, she could see a narrow balcony with a wrought iron railing.

"Hey, come on in here," Ned called from the kitchen.

Nancy and Brenda hurried into the brightly lit room. A few dishes were in the sink, but otherwise it was clean. Ned pointed to a calendar stuck on the refrigerator door.

"I think I just solved the case!" he said.

Nancy peered closer. Ned's finger marked Friday the fourteenth, the previous day. "Blaine—dinner at Winters" was written in the square along with a three o'clock appointment at R.H. Diagnostics.

"Let me see," Brenda said, pushing past Nancy.

"Could be they decided to spend the weekend together," Nancy said.

Brenda straightened abruptly. "That note proves nothing. Pam would have canceled our lunch date for today."

Nancy sighed. "All right. We'll check out the rest of the apartment."

Ned and Brenda followed Nancy as she quickly looked in Pam's bedroom and office. Everything seemed in place.

"Definitely no sign of foul play," Ned said as they walked back to the living room.

"I guess you're right," Brenda reluctantly agreed.

The loud ringing of the phone made all three jump.

"Hello, this is five-five-five, seven-oh-three-oh," a female voice said. Nancy remembered the answering machine in Pam's office. "Please leave a message at the tone."

Nancy held her breath, wondering if the caller would leave a message, but a loud click told her the person had hung up.

"Let's check out the messages on the machine," Nancy suggested as she headed down the hall and into Pam's office.

"Isn't that being pretty nosy?" Ned asked as he and Brenda followed.

"Sure," Brenda replied. "But Pam would understand. Look, two messages." She pressed Rewind, then Play Back. Nancy stood with her arms crossed, slightly annoyed at how quickly Brenda had taken over.

"Maybe the messages will give us a clue to where Pam is," Brenda said.

The voice on the first message was muffled. "Pam, this is Blaine. It's five o'clock. I'm at a contractor's office and can't be reached. I need you to meet me at the job site at seven."

"See?" Ned said from the doorway. "I told you. Case closed."

"Shh," Nancy hushed him. "Let's listen to the second message."

"Pam! It's Blaine. Where are you?" This time the voice was clear and sounded very angry. "It's ten o'clock Friday night. You'd better have a good explanation for not showing up tonight for our date!"

Chapter Two

A LOUD CLICK signaled that Blaine had hung up. Nancy shot Ned a surprised look. If Pam hadn't met Blaine for their date, then where was she?

"I told you," Brenda announced triumphantly as she pressed the Save button on the machine. "Something's definitely wrong if Pam's been missing since last night."

Nancy frowned at Brenda. It almost sounded as if she were *glad* Pam was missing. "Okay, so something's a little odd. But let's not panic."

Ned crossed his arms. "Nancy's right. Someone should call this Blaine guy and find out if he's seen Pam since he left the second message. She may have just been late for their date."

Brenda snorted. "Three hours late? Come on,

guys, you just don't want to admit that I'm right. Pam *is* missing."

But Nancy was already checking Pam's desk for a phone and address book. When she found one, she opened it to the *Y*s and found Blaine's home number. It was a Chicago exchange.

"Okay, Brenda. First thing you need to do is call Pam's boyfriend and find out if Pam's there. Ned may be right."

As Brenda dialed, Ned pulled Nancy into the hall. "Maybe Brenda has Pam tied up in the trunk of her car just so she can get a story."

Nancy smothered a giggle. "That sounds like something Brenda would do. Still, we'd better take this seriously."

"Blaine! I'm so glad I got you!" Brenda said into the phone. She gestured wildly to Nancy to listen in. Nancy stepped closer so that when Brenda tipped the receiver, she could hear a male voice.

"Who is this?" Blaine Young asked.

"Brenda Carlton from *Today's Times*. I've been trying to get in touch with Pam. Do you know where she is?"

"No!" Blaine retorted. "And at this point I don't care. This is the last time she stands me up!"

"You mean she never met you at the River Heights job site?"

"What are you talking about? I was in Chicago last night. We were supposed to meet at Winters restaurant, but she never showed up."

Nancy's eyes widened. For a second she covered the mouthpiece with her hand. "Ask him about the first message," she whispered to Brenda.

"But, Blaine," Brenda protested. "Last night you left a message on Pam's answering machine to meet you at seven at the River Heights job site."

"What are you talking about?" Blaine replied. "I didn't leave any such message. But I do have a message for Pam. You tell her this is the last time I play second fiddle to one of her big stories!" Without a goodbye, he hung up.

"What a jerk," Brenda said.

Nancy tapped her lip in thought. "If Blaine didn't leave that message, then who did? The voice on the tape was muffled, so it will be hard to tell."

"It is weird," Brenda said as she slowly replaced the phone receiver. "And why would someone else send Pam to the job site where Blaine's working?"

Nancy shook her head. "I don't know, but something tells me we'd better find out. Brenda, do you know where this job site is?"

"Yes, I dropped Pam off there once. Blaine's company designed the new building being constructed in the center of town."

"River Heights's tallest skyscraper?" Ned asked.

"Right. Twenty stories high," Brenda said.

"Let's drive over and see if there was a guard who saw Pam there last night," Nancy said.

When Nancy set the address book back on the desk, she noticed a snapshot stuck in the blotter. She picked it up and studied the picture. A handsome, dark-haired guy was slouched against a sports car, his arm around Pam Harter's shoulders. Pam had a confident expression, long, blond hair, and the figure of a model. Ned's right, Nancy thought—the reporter is gorgeous.

"That's Mr. Hotshot himself," Brenda said over Nancy's shoulder. "His company, High Designs, has really been in demand this past year. That's one reason why Pam and Blaine had their ups and downs. They were both obsessed with their careers, so they rarely saw each other. Then he took an apartment in Chicago. Pam thought that if she landed a really big story, one of the Chicago papers would hire her. Then she could be with him more."

"I think I'll borrow this," Nancy said, sliding the photo into her shoulder bag. "Just in case this really does turn into a mystery."

"Hmmph," Brenda said as she swept from the room, her purse whacking Ned on the arm. "As far as I'm concerned, this already is a mystery."

Twenty minutes later Ned steered the car along the construction site. A high chain-link fence surrounded it. Nancy could see tall beams jutting into the night sky. The partially erected building looked like a giant skeleton. Around the building, the muddy grounds were dotted with piles of building materials and large construction equipment.

Nancy's stomach tightened as she studied the area inside the fence. It was dark, deserted, and dangerous—a perfect place for a crime, she thought grimly.

Ned braked when he came to the entrance. Two wide gates were padlocked together. "Doesn't look like Pam could've got in. And there's no guard on duty."

"She could have driven in on Friday before the crews left," Nancy said.

"So *we've* got to go in there," Brenda stated emphatically from the backseat.

"At least we need to see if Pam's car is around." Turning, Nancy opened the car door. Brenda climbed out the backseat.

While Ned parked the car out of sight, the two girls walked slowly down the length of chain fence. Nancy kept her gaze glued to the construction site.

"What color is Pam's car?" she asked.

"Ooooh, yuck." Brenda stopped beside her. The heel of one leather flat was stuck in gooey, reddish brown mud. "It's the car in the photo—the neon blue sporty job."

Nancy pulled her penlight from her bag and shone the weak beam through the fence. Ned jogged up behind her, carrying a large flashlight.

"Aren't you glad I'm prepared?" he teased.

Flicking it on, he aimed the bright light on a stack of steel rods, then slowly moved it past a backhoe and bulldozer.

"Stop there." Nancy caught his arm. She'd glimpsed a flash of blue behind the bulldozer's blade.

"It looks like the trunk and taillight of a sports car," Ned said.

"Brenda?" Nancy called. Brenda was standing on a patch of grass, trying to scrape the mud off her shoe. "Come look at this."

Grumbling about the mud, Brenda hobbled up and peered through the fence. She gasped and clapped her hand to her mouth. "That's Pam's car!"

"I think one of us should find a phone and call the police," Nancy suggested quickly.

Ned tossed Brenda his keys. "Brenda can go—I'm not letting you climb in there alone, Nancy."

"What makes you think I'm going in there?" Nancy asked, but she was already moving along the fence, trying to find a place to climb over.

"No way. I'm not leaving," Brenda declared, throwing the keys back to Ned. "If Pam is in there, you're not beating me out of a scoop, Nancy Drew."

Nancy spun around to glare at Brenda. "Aren't you the least bit concerned about your friend?"

Brenda flushed. "Of course. That was the second reason why I wasn't leaving."

"Hey, there're a few concrete blocks," Nancy

said. Picking one up, she set it down in front of the fence. "Ned, if I stand on two of these, can you boost me the rest of the way?"

"In your dress and trench coat?" Ned sounded doubtful.

But Nancy had already stacked the second block on top of the first. Clinging to the chain-link fence, she climbed on top of the blocks. Ned put his hands under her bent knee, then lifted her up. Nancy grasped the top of the fence and pulled herself up until she was draped over the top.

"Ouch, this hurts," she grunted. She swung her leg over, then awkwardly hunted for a toehold so she could climb down the other side.

"We won't *have* to call the police," Ned said. "Any minute they'll find us—breaking in!"

"I'll just flash my press badge," Brenda said smugly. "Here, Nickerson." She flipped her shoulder bag strap around Ned's neck, then climbed to the top of the blocks, using his shoulder for a handhold. "Now boost me over."

Minutes later the three were finally inside the construction site. Using Ned's flashlight, Nancy led the way toward the rear of the blue car. It was parked between the bulldozer and the construction office trailer.

Nancy stopped at the back fender and shone the light into the car. It reflected off the windshield. Still, she could see a dark mound on the driver's side. The sight made her heart race.

Brenda dug her nails into Nancy's wrist. "This

is Pam's car all right—and it looks like someone's in there!"

"Or something," Ned said in a low voice.

Nancy nodded once, then quickly moved around to the driver's side. Holding her breath, she aimed the flashlight through the rolled-down window.

The yellow light bounced off pale skin. A woman was slumped behind the steering wheel, her head lolling back on the seat. Two unblinking eyes stared at the car's ceiling. The woman's mouth hung slack. Blond hair cascaded around the shoulders.

Nancy choked back a gasp. "It's Pam," she said, the words catching in her throat.

Behind Nancy, Brenda let out a strangled cry and twisted away. Ned came up beside Nancy.

"Is she—" His unfinished question hung in the air.

Slowly Nancy reached out and touched Pam's pale cheek. The skin was cold.

She nodded. Tears filled her eyes. "Yes," Nancy whispered. "Pam Harter's dead."

Chapter Three

"OUR FIRST CALL," Frank Hardy announced as he steered the River Heights Rescue Squad ambulance around several cars. Siren blaring, Frank slowed, checked to make sure traffic had stopped, then sped through a red light.

"And it sounds like a good one!" Joe said excitedly. Blue eyes wide, he stared out the windshield as buildings and streetlights flashed by. A book of maps lay open on his lap.

Frank shot him a puzzled look. "You think a possible priority four—a dead person—is a good call?"

"Better than sitting around the squad building for another night," Joe said. The two brothers were wearing white coveralls with "River Heights

Rescue Squad" stitched over the pocket. "I'm ready for some excitement."

"You mean tracking down body snatchers isn't exciting enough?" Frank teased his younger brother.

Chief McGinnis had called in the Hardys after two bodies, on two different occasions, had been stolen from rescue squad ambulances. The bodies had been on their way to the hospital to be officially declared dead.

Joe grimaced. "This case is more weird than exciting. I mean, can you figure out why anyone would want to steal a dead body from an ambulance?"

"No," Frank admitted. "But neither can McGinnis and the River Heights Police Department." He glanced at Joe. "What do *you* think?"

Joe curled back his upper lip. His face looked blue in the streetlights. "Vampires," he said in a ghoulish voice.

Frank laughed. "Sure. Hey, there's the construction site." He pointed out the windshield to a fenced-in area. A huge sign said Gatlin Brothers Construction Company.

"Turn right," Joe said to Frank. "The Nine-one-one dispatcher said the gates were off Main Street."

Frank hung a fast right and saw a flashing police light ahead. A uniformed officer waved the ambulance through an open gate in a chain-link fence.

As Frank steered the vehicle through the gates, he had to admit that his adrenaline was up, too. They'd been taking a course in school on emergency care, but when Chief McGinnis had called for their help, they'd also taken a crash course to prepare for the emergency medical technician's exam. Going on their first call was exciting.

The ambulance bounced through potholes and over debris. Joe's hand was on the dashboard for support. Frank steered toward a police car parked next to an unmarked car. The flashing red light on top reflected off construction vehicles and supplies.

"Think we're too late?" Joe asked. A uniformed female officer suddenly stepped in front of the ambulance, gesturing them to stop.

"Maybe not!" Frank exclaimed. Parking quickly, he pulled two disposable gloves from the dispenser between the seats, grabbed the primary bag that held all their necessary supplies, and jumped from the unit. Joe climbed out the other side.

"Over here," the police officer called as she led the Hardys around a bulldozer. A dark-haired girl about Frank's age was stretched out on a grassy spot, her head propped on a coat.

"She passed out," the officer explained. "Her pulse and respiration are fine."

"This isn't the victim called in by the dispatcher?" Frank asked.

The officer shook her head. "No." She nodded

toward a blue sports car. Yellow crime-scene tape circled the area around the car. Several people were hovering around it checking for physical evidence. "The one in there is definitely dead."

Frank squatted by the girl's side. She had pale skin and long, dark lashes.

"Joe, you check her blood pressure while I take her pulse," Frank said, picking up her limp wrist.

Just then the girl's lashes fluttered and her eyes opened. When she saw Frank hovering over her, she let out a piercing scream.

Frank was so startled, he dropped her wrist.

Gently Joe pressed down on the girl's shoulder. "It's all right. We're emergency medical technicians from the River Heights Rescue Squad," he explained in a calm voice. "We've been trained to provide emergency care."

"Oh." The girl struggled to push herself up on her elbows. She had wide, dark eyes.

Very pretty, Frank thought, but I think she's going to be a real pain. "My name is Frank Hardy," he said. "The police officer said you passed out. You shouldn't get up until we check you over."

The girl frowned at him. "Get away. I'm fine."

"Please, miss, we're trained to help," Joe repeated. "We'd like to check your blood pressure and ask you some questions that will help us determine if you really *are* fine. Can you tell me what day it is?"

The girl shot him an annoyed look. "It's Saturday. Do you think I'm a moron? Now get away." Raising up, she pushed Joe aside and pulled the raincoat over her knees. "Nancy!" she hollered.

Nancy? Frank glanced over his shoulder and saw two people talking. Frank immediately recognized both Nancy and Chief McGinnis, head of the police department.

What was Nancy Drew doing here?

"Frank! Joe!" When Nancy saw the two brothers, she hurried over. Though Frank could tell she was glad to see them, he saw worry lines between her brows. He also noticed that her trench coat was streaked with dirt and her stockings had runs up both legs. Nancy was obviously involved in whatever was going on.

"Nancy, you know these two?" the dark-haired girl on the ground asked.

"Uh." Nancy stopped in her tracks. Frank caught his breath. He hoped she wouldn't blow their cover.

"Yes," Nancy said smoothly. "Joe and Frank Hardy taught a CPR course I took last year. Joe, Frank—meet Brenda Carlton, a reporter from *Today's Times.*"

Frank glanced down at the girl, who was frowning as if she didn't believe Nancy's story.

"Hello, Brenda." Frank held out his hand to shake hers. "Now that we've been formally introduced, can my brother do a quick check to make sure you're all right?"

Almost coyly, Brenda lowered her lashes, then looked up at Frank. "Oh, all right," she said.

"But I really am fine. It's just that a friend of mine was . . ."—her voice faltered—"murdered. I took it pretty hard."

"And that's a good reason to check you over," Joe said, picking up the blood pressure cuff.

Frank stood and walked a few feet away with Nancy. He slipped his arm over her shoulder so he could whisper in her ear.

"What's going on?" he asked. "We got a call from the dispatcher to rush over here to check out a possible priority four and we find you!"

"Pam Harter, who's also a reporter for the *Times,* is dead," Nancy explained. "Brenda came to me tonight because she suspected something. We found Pam in her car. She was—"

"Why, hello, Frank," a deep, male voice cut in.

Frank snapped his head around. Ned Nickerson, Nancy's boyfriend, stood behind the two. Frank had met him several times on other cases. Hands shoved in his pockets, head cocked, Ned seemed to be sizing Frank up.

"Hi, Ned." Frank dropped his arm from around Nancy's shoulder. "I'm not going to act too friendly since Brenda Carlton's keeping an eagle eye on us." He nodded toward Joe and Brenda. His brother was asking Brenda some questions, but her attention was directed at Nancy and Frank.

"I'm not surprised Brenda's curious about what you're doing," Ned said. "In fact, I thought when we found Pam, Brenda was going to whip out a camera and take pictures. Instead, she got hysterical and fainted. Luckily, I was able to flag down a police officer, and he immediately radioed for help."

"It *has* been a crazy night," Nancy said with a tired sigh. "At first Ned and I didn't believe Brenda's story about Pam disappearing. Brenda's been known to exaggerate."

"What do the police think happened to Pam?" Frank asked.

"Come here." Nancy gestured for Frank and Ned to follow her toward the blue car. They stopped in front of the yellow tape that was stretched around the car. Frank could see the dead woman slumped in the front seat. A man crouched beside the body, placing a plastic bag over the victim's left hand. A woman wearing jeans and a nylon jacket was taking photos.

Frank had seen many dead people. Still, he swallowed hard.

"See the bruises on her throat?" Nancy asked. "It appears she was strangled."

"Strangled?" Frank repeated. "While she was sitting in her car? And what was she doing parked inside the construction site?"

Nancy and Ned quickly told him about Brenda's suspicions, checking out the apartment, the phone message, and Brenda's call to Blaine Young.

"The medical examiner says rigor mortis was actually starting to lessen," Nancy added. "That means she was killed over twenty-four hours ago. That could be any time before early Friday night.

"McGinnis and I discovered several other things, too," Nancy continued. She pointed to the window on the driver's side. "The window was rolled down—as if she had been talking to someone."

Frank's eyes widened. "The suspect strangled her through the window?"

"No. The passenger-side door was ajar, and there's mud from the site on the floor—as if someone had been in the car with her."

Frank whistled. "Wow. Was there a sign of a struggle?"

"Not much. The crime technician's checking for evidence now. But if there wasn't a struggle, that narrows down the list of suspects."

"Right," Frank agreed. "Pam Harter must have met someone she knew."

"Someone she trusted enough to let in her car and drive to this secluded spot," Nancy said. "If you ask me, all the evidence points to Blaine Young. I think Pam's boyfriend could be the murderer!"

Chapter Four

"Of course Blaine Young killed Pam Harter!" a shrill voice cried out behind Nancy.

Nancy spun around. Brenda's dark eyes flashed from Frank to Ned to Nancy.

"Brenda, I was just saying that the evidence merely suggests—" Nancy started to say.

"Suggests!" Brenda exclaimed. "I'd say the evidence is as obvious as a neon sign. I always told Pam that Blaine was a conceited jerk."

Nancy took a deep breath. "Brenda, that doesn't mean he killed her. The police will have to look at all the evidence and—"

Brenda snorted. "*I* have all the evidence I need. And as for motive—I'll bet Pam Harter was killed because she dug up some real dirt on Blaine and his company."

Nancy's eyes widened. "What are you talking about?"

"Don't you read the papers, Nancy?" Brenda smiled smugly. "There have been hints that the companies working on this high rise were cutting corners. Pam could have found something out and threatened to write an article exposing the fraud. And that's what I'm going to write in my own story—that Blaine Young killed his girlfriend to silence her. Now if you'll excuse me, I've got an exclusive to call in to the *Times.*"

Whipping her purse strap onto her shoulder, Brenda stormed away.

Ned and Frank stared after her. Finally Frank turned to Nancy. "Is she really going to write an article saying that Blaine Young killed Pam?"

Nancy shrugged. "Probably. Fortunately her father—he's the owner of the paper—knows to edit everything she writes before it gets printed. Otherwise the paper would have a million lawsuits."

"Will someone tell me what's going on?" Joe asked as he joined the group.

Nancy and Ned filled him in.

"My hunch is that Blaine left that first message saying that Pam should meet him," Nancy said. "He killed her Friday night, knowing that no one would discover her body until Monday morning when the crews showed up for work."

"I bet he left the second message to throw the police off," Ned added.

"But why would Blaine kill his own girlfriend?" Frank asked.

Nancy shrugged. "I hate to admit that Brenda may be right. When I read Pam's articles, I got the feeling she was the kind of reporter who felt obligated to write the truth—even if it meant hurting her boyfriend's company."

Frank shook his head. "Nothing like coming to River Heights and finding ourselves involved in two mysteries."

"So what's going on with your assignment?" Nancy asked.

"Not much," Joe answered. "When Chief McGinnis first told us about missing bodies and hijacked ambulances, I thought, Wow. This will be straight out of a horror movie! But on the two nights we've been on duty, the worst thing I've encountered is the squad room coffee."

Ned and Nancy laughed.

"I'm just wondering if being on a squad is the best way to ferret out these body snatchers," Frank said. "But McGinnis seems to think it's an inside job, so he wants us to keep an eye on the other crew members."

Just then the medical examiner called to Chief McGinnis. Nancy quickly excused herself. "I want to hear this," she said.

Stepping over the tape, the medical examiner held up a clear plastic bag for Chief McGinnis to inspect. Frowning, McGinnis studied the contents. Nancy could see it was a small, white rectangle of paper.

"I found it clutched in her left hand," the examiner told McGinnis. "It's an appointment card for a place called R.H. Diagnostics. Her purse was open and her hand stuck inside, as if she reached for the card at the last minute. Since the rigor mortis was loosening, I was able to pull the card from between her fingers."

Nancy and McGinnis exchanged glances.

"Interesting," McGinnis said. "Was there a date and time on it?"

"No."

Nancy suddenly remembered Pam's calendar. "There was a note on Pam's calendar for a three o'clock appointment at R.H. Diagnostics on Friday."

"I'll have the detectives check it out," McGinnis said.

When the examiner went back to her work, McGinnis pulled Nancy aside. "How's Brenda?" he asked.

Nancy bit back a smile. "Ready to wrap up your case."

He sighed wearily. "When I saw that Brenda had passed out, I called her father. He should be here any minute. I'll have to warn him to keep an eye on her story. There are certain things we don't need to leak to the public." Tilting his head, he nodded toward the Hardys. "They're on a tough assignment, Nan. State Representative Margaret Cavallo is really breathing down my neck. One of the bodies stolen from the ambulance belonged to her half brother, Sam Cavallo."

"I never got to hear the whole story. How did it happen?" Nancy asked, intrigued by the report of body snatchers.

"According to the EMTs who were on duty that night, they responded to a one A.M. call—a car crash. Sam Cavallo had lost control of his car on a rain-slick road. The EMTs couldn't resuscitate him. The ambulance was on its way to the hospital—a doctor has to pronounce a person dead—when the EMTs received a second call of a car accident nearby. When they stopped to check out the alleged accident, two people in ski masks jumped them. They tied the EMTs up, blindfolded and gagged them, and locked them in the back of the ambulance. When the local police officer found them, the only thing missing was Sam Cavallo's body."

"Wow. That is some story," Nancy said, shivering. "And all this happened a week ago?"

McGinnis nodded. Dark circles ringed his eyes. Pam Harter's murder would only add to the police chief's stress. Nancy wondered if he'd had any sleep the last couple of nights.

"The first body was snatched a week before that. It was another man—James Squire. He was divorced, and his wife and relatives live in Arizona, so there wasn't such an uproar. But now with the second theft, we worry there's a pattern."

"That means if there is a pattern, body number three could be stolen any day," Nancy added grimly.

"Right. We have no idea why someone is stealing bodies. We do know whoever took them was a professional—they left no evidence. The Hardys have really got to be on their toes. Otherwise they could be in great danger!"

"Well, that was an exciting call," Joe said. He slouched in the passenger seat of the ambulance, his eyes closed. The siren was silent as Frank drove slowly back to the squad headquarters.

It was one in the morning. Since Joe and Frank were hired as part of the rescue squad's night crew, Joe knew he'd have to get used to responding to calls at all hours. Still, now that the adrenaline rush was over, he was feeling plain old tired.

"Not that we got to do much," he added with a yawn. "That Brenda was something."

"Imagine running into Nancy *and* a mystery on our second night here in River Heights," Frank said.

Joe snorted. "You mean *another* mystery. We're already investigating one, remember? So forget about Pam Harter's murder. We've got to figure out who stole two dead people from this ambulance." He shook his head. "It still sounds too weird to believe."

"Oh, I believe it, all right," Frank said. "If we can figure out 'why' someone would want bodies, maybe that will lead us to the 'who.'"

Opening one eye, Joe peered at Frank. "Okay,

we've got a few minutes before we get back to the squad. Why would someone stop an ambulance and steal a body headed for the morgue?"

Frank shrugged. "In the old days, grave robbers sold bodies to scientists and doctors."

"It's hard to believe that could happen today." Joe shuddered. "Besides, today people can donate their bodies to science." He rubbed his eyes and yawned. "Maybe if we can figure out who on the squad is in cahoots with the 'ambulance-jackers,' we'll get a lead. Any ideas on how to ferret out these bad guys?" Joe added as the ambulance turned into the drive of the rescue squad.

The square, brick building had a flagpole out front. The drive curved around back where two large garage doors and one regular door led to the lower level.

"No. I'm too tired to think." Frank yawned so wide his jaw cracked. "This running around after midnight is tough work. That bunk at the squad is going to feel good."

"You're telling me." Joe pressed the button on the garage door opener.

The door rumbled open. A second ambulance, Unit No. 51, was parked in the garage.

"Jessica and Luke must have returned from their call already," Frank noted as he pulled the ambulance carefully into the bay.

Jessica Gallagher and Luke Kao were the other paid emergency medical technicians on the night squad. Luke, the night crew leader, had shown the Hardys around when they had first arrived and introduced them to some of the day crew members.

Joe opened the ambulance door and swung his long legs out. The fluorescent lights made his eyes water. "I'll check the supplies in back to make sure everything's okay," he told Frank.

"Great," Frank said. "I'll head to the office and start filling out the call sheet."

Joe trudged to the back of the ambulance. He was reaching for the handle when he noticed that the back door of Ambulance No. 51 was open a crack.

That's weird, he thought. Both Jessica and Luke had stressed how important it was that the ambulances were put away checked and ready for the next call. An open back door would be hazardous when a crew zoomed from the garage.

Well, maybe I'll just close it without saying anything, Joe thought. They were probably tired.

Stepping closer, he reached out to close the door when suddenly it flew wide open, slamming him in the chest. With a startled cry, Joe flew backward and hit the concrete floor. At the same time, someone hurtled from the ambulance and dashed out of sight around the side of the ambulance.

"Hey!" Joe hollered, leaping to his feet. Instantly he winced. Grabbing his aching back, he hobbled to the front of the garage, just in time to hear the exit door slam.

When he reached the door and ran outside, he

saw no one. There wasn't even the sound of a car driving off.

What in the world was that all about? Joe wondered. He turned and checked the back door. The lock hadn't been tampered with, which meant the person had most likely used a key.

Joe relocked the door, then, ignoring the ache in his back, he hurried to Ambulance No. 51. Had someone been messing with the supplies?

Quickly he climbed in and checked the medical equipment and supplies. Nothing seemed out of place. Still he'd have to alert the day crew to do an extra-thorough job when they checked off the equipment in the morning.

As Joe stepped from the ambulance, he stopped to think about the intruder. The person had a bulky build—too bulky for a female, Joe decided, unless the women's football team was in town. And he'd worn a ski mask. Still, it had to be someone who had a key to the outside door, and that narrowed it down to a member of the squad. But why would someone who worked there want to mess with an ambulance?

Joe shrugged as he headed back to his unit, No. 53. When he'd finished checking the supplies, he made sure the keys were in the ignitions of both ambulances and the doors unlocked. Then he turned off the garage lights and went upstairs.

A long hall bisected the first floor. Joe walked past the squad's kitchen, the women's locker room and bunk room, and the men's locker room. He was so tired, he decided not even to bother washing up or undressing. He'd wait until later to tell Frank about the intruder.

It was almost two in the morning. The night shift ended at six A.M. That meant, if he fell asleep right now, and there wasn't another call, he could get four hours of sleep.

Joe groaned. Four hours!

Quietly he opened the door to the men's bunk room. It was dark. A bulge in the right-hand bed told him that Luke was already sacked out. He glanced at the middle bed that Frank had claimed. It was empty.

Yawning, Joe stumbled toward the bed on the far left side. It would feel so—

Wait a second. Joe stopped in his tracks. Through bleary eyes, he noticed that the left-hand bed had a bulge in it, too. Someone was sleeping in his bed!

That didn't make sense. Luke had assigned him that bed, and he was going to lie down, no matter what.

Then Joe remembered the intruder. What if the person hadn't tampered only with the ambulance? What if something else strange was going on?

Joe tensed, the thought jarring him awake. Cautiously he approached the bed. His eyes had adjusted to the dark, and he could see a head almost entirely covered by the blanket.

I'll just surprise whoever it is, Joe told himself

as he got closer. Reaching out, he took hold of the blanket and pulled it away.

Startled, Joe jumped backward.

Someone *was* in his bed—a man, lying on his back, with a knife handle sticking up out of his chest!

Chapter Five

A GUY'S BEEN STABBED in my bed! Joe thought wildly. Staggering backward, he groped along the wall until he found the light switch. He flicked the light on at the same instant Luke Kao shot bolt upright in his bunk.

"What in the world is going on, Hardy?" he cried angrily. "Turn off that light. I'm trying to sleep."

Behind Joe, the door swung open. Frank blinked in the doorway. "What's going on in here?"

Joe pointed to his bed. "I'll tell you what's going on. Someone's in my bed—and he's been stabbed!" Now that the light was on, he could see the knife clearly. The person didn't move.

"Who's been stabbed?" A female voice asked next to Joe. Jessica Gallagher, the fourth night crew member, stood beside him, her mouth open as she stared at the bed. Jessica was in her twenties. She had short, red hair, freckles, and broad shoulders, and was wearing a baggy sweatshirt and sweatpants.

Together, Joe, Frank, and Jessica approached the bed. Mumbling about not getting any sleep, Luke swung his legs to the floor and joined them.

When Joe got a closer look at the person in his bed, he scowled. "That's not a person. That's a dummy!" Snapping his head around, Joe glared at Luke. "Who put a dummy in my bed?"

Joe heard a muffled snort. Turning, he stared at Jessica. Her hand was clapped over her mouth as she choked back her giggles.

"I did." She laughed. "When you were out on your call. As a joke."

Luke and Frank started to laugh.

"And I added the knife," Luke said. "The dummy is Rescue Ralph. The squad uses him to practice CPR and rescue techniques."

Jessica touched Joe's arm. His fists were still clenched at his sides. "Are you all right?" she asked. "We didn't mean to freak you out. Every new crew member gets the same initiation."

"Yeah, he's fine." Frank clapped Joe on the back. "That's the kind of prank Joe loves to pull."

Joe shook his head. "Actually, it is pretty funny," he admitted. "Any other time I would have died laughing. It's just that before I came upstairs, I surprised somebody snooping around in the garage."

Instantly Jessica, Frank, and Luke quit laughing. "What are you talking about?" Luke asked.

Joe told everyone what had happened.

"Man. I hope it's not connected to this body snatching thing," Luke said. "We're already getting enough heat from Captain Graham, Chief McGinnis, and the press."

"Yeah. We read about that," Frank said. "Any idea what's going on?"

Jessica shook her head. "None. The two crew members, Mike and Renee, who were ambushed and tied up, were put on day duty until further investigation. That's why you guys were hired." Jessica snorted. "Mike and Renee were both furious. Day duty is strictly volunteer. So it's like they were suspended from their paid job. They swear they had nothing to do with the body snatchings. They think they've been made scapegoats."

"That's Mike Hosford and Renee Torres?" Joe asked, remembering their names from Captain Graham's briefing. He'd also met Renee when Luke had introduced several members of the day crew.

"Right." Luke ran his fingers through his straight, black hair. "I agree with Jessica. Graham dropped them from the night crew without even listening to their stories. I don't blame them for being mad."

Joe and Frank exchanged glances. It didn't sound as though Luke or Jessica thought their fellow crew members could have been involved with the body snatchings. Still, the EMTs were likely suspects, and Joe couldn't help but wonder if either Renee or Mike had broken into the ambulance. Both of them had access to the garage.

"Well, that's enough excitement for tonight," Luke said. Reaching down, he pulled Rescue Ralph from under the blanket. Then he held the dummy in front of him and stuck the plastic hand out to Joe.

"Can we shake and be friends?" Luke asked in a phony voice.

Joe rolled his eyes and grinned. "Friends," he agreed, gingerly shaking Ralph's hand.

Jessica laughed. "Welcome to the night shift, Joe and Frank Hardy. Where *anything* can happen."

"What are you going to order, Nan?" Ned asked early the next afternoon.

"Umm." Nancy scanned the menu. "I don't know. Everything looks wonderful. I heard the Sunday brunch at Winters is out of this world."

"So are the prices," Ned said.

With a laugh, Nancy closed her menu and waved at the wall-length picture window they were seated next to. "But look at the view! It's definitely worth it."

Winters was located on the top floor of one of

Chicago's five-star hotels. From her seat, Nancy could see past the towering skyscrapers of downtown Chicago to Lake Michigan far below.

"Besides"—Nancy leaned forward, a teasing grin on her lips—"this is my treat."

Ned's expression brightened. "Oh, good. Then in that case, I'll order steak and eggs, juice—"

"Boy, investigating a murder really gives you an appetite," Nancy joked.

Ned closed his menu, too, and picked up his cup of coffee. "Talking about investigating—how are you going to find out if Blaine was here Friday night?"

"With your help, it'll be easy," Nancy said as she reached for the basket of popovers and blueberry muffins.

Half an hour later, Nancy was finishing the last bite of her vegetable omelet. When the waiter came by, she asked for more hot tea. In an instant, he returned and filled her cup. Nancy lifted a few ice cubes from her water glass to help cool it.

"That was a perfect steak," Ned said, settling back in his seat. "I guess this makes up for that romantic dinner we didn't eat last night. Thank you." Smiling, he leaned across the table and tilted his head to kiss her.

Nancy leaned toward him. As their lips touched, Nancy's elbow hit the hot tea. The full cup spilled on the tablecloth and streamed onto Ned's lap.

With a loud yelp, he jumped from his seat,

hitting the table with his hip and knocking over Nancy's water glass. Ice-cold water spewed all over Nancy, the table, and the floor.

"Oh, Ned!" Nancy cried. Jumping up, she dabbed furiously at his soaked shirt and pants. "Waiter! Waiter!" she called excitedly. "More napkins—please!"

The staff sprang into action. Even the maitre d' charged over, extra linens in hand.

"Oh, I'm so sorry, Ned," Nancy apologized. Ned was frowning at her. She bit back a grin. Okay, so he knew she'd done it on purpose.

Grabbing her shoulder bag, Nancy dodged the waiters. "I'm going to the ladies' room," she called. When she reached the entrance to the restaurant, she glanced right and left. Everyone was helping to mop up the mess.

Quickly she opened the reservation book to Friday night and ran her index finger down the entries. There it was: "Young—party of two." The reservation time was for eight-thirty, but there was no check mark beside it, even though all the other names had check marks beside them.

That meant Blaine had had a reservation but hadn't kept it. That made sense since Pam hadn't shown up. But had he even been at Winters? Or was he back at River Heights—committing a murder!

Whipping the picture of Blaine and Pam from her purse, Nancy entered the quiet bar area. A lone bartender was minding the curved, mahogany bar. He stopped polishing a glass to smile at Nancy.

"Need a napkin?" he asked, nodding at Nancy's stained pants leg.

She shook her head as she slid onto the barstool. "No, what I do need is help identifying someone." She pushed the picture across the bar. "Do you remember seeing this guy Friday night? He had a reservation for dinner at eight-thirty."

The bartender raised one brow. "And why do you want to know?"

Nancy looked down. "He's my boyfriend," she said. "And I think he had a date with another woman—this woman." She pointed to Pam.

"Oh, too bad." The bartender set down the glass and studied the picture for a minute. "Yeah, he was here. I can't be sure of the time. I think it was about nine o'clock. Hung around, then left. In fact, I remember him complaining that his date stood him up."

The bartender smiled when he handed her back the picture. "Sounds to me like you ought to ditch the bum. Especially since you're better-looking than the chick in the picture," he added with a grin.

Nancy smiled back as she thanked him. The bartender was cute—or as Bess would say, a real hunk.

As she went into the ladies' room, Nancy mulled over the information. Blaine had been at

Winters at nine o'clock. It took an hour and a half to drive from River Heights to Chicago. He could have killed Pam around seven and still made it to Winters to establish an alibi.

Ned was staring at the check when Nancy returned to the table.

"All dry?" she asked as she slid into her seat.

"Soaking wet." He rolled his eyes. "Pretty smooth move, Nan. I hope you got the information you needed."

"I did. I'll tell you all about it in the car. We need to get back to River Heights and call McGinnis. I want to ask him if the medical examiner has determined what time Pam Harter was killed."

Reaching across the table, Nancy plucked the check from Ned's fingers. "My treat, remember? And you deserve it." She laughed when Ned stood up. The whole front of his pants was damp. "I guess I should pay for dry cleaning your pants, too. I couldn't have found out this information without your help."

Two hours later Ned turned the car into Nancy's drive. Before he turned off the motor, Hannah Gruen, the Drew's longtime housekeeper, came out of the house, pulling her sweater around her shoulders. Nancy quickly opened the car door.

"What's the matter?" she asked the older woman.

"Brenda Carlton called about half an hour ago," Hannah said. "She wants you to meet her at the *Times* at six o'clock. She'll leave the front door unlocked."

"I'll bet she found out something about Pam!" Nancy said excitedly.

"Pam Harter?" Hannah asked. "The reporter who was killed?"

Nancy nodded. Then she noticed the Hardys' rental car parked at the curb. "Say hi to Joe and Frank before they leave for their night shift," she told Hannah.

The housekeeper grinned. "It might be a while. They have to eat early, so right now they're polishing off a whole roast chicken and an entire bowl of mashed potatoes!"

Nancy laughed. After thanking Hannah, she shut the car door. "Mind going to *Today's Times* with me at six?" she asked Ned.

"Sure. But first let's head to my house. I want to change into some jeans," he said as he backed the car from the drive. "Then we'll see what Brenda wants. I'm as curious as you are."

The sky was gray with clouds when Ned parked across the street from the *Times* building. Brenda's car was parked out front. Several lights were on inside the building, but it still looked deserted.

Nancy jumped out and, after waiting for Ned, crossed the street. A light, chilly rain had started to fall.

"Brenda?" Nancy called when she and Ned stepped into the receptionist area. Since it was a

Sunday evening, the building was empty. Nancy hadn't been in the *Times* for quite a while and didn't know where Brenda's office was located.

Suddenly the building was plunged into darkness.

"What's going on?" Ned asked. "There wasn't a storm predicted for tonight."

"I don't know," Nancy said tersely. "But I hope this isn't Brenda's idea of a joke." She reached inside her purse for her penlight.

Suddenly they heard a loud moan.

Nancy grabbed Ned's arm. "Ned, that must be Brenda!"

Chapter Six

BRENDA!" Nancy screamed. "Where are you? Are you all right?"

Holding her penlight in front of her, Nancy hurried down the hall toward the sound of the moan.

"Brenda!" Ned's deep voice rang out.

For a second the two stopped to listen. The building was silent.

"Do you know where her office is?" Ned asked.

"No. We've got to keep looking."

They entered a large room sectioned off into cubicles. Ned reached for the light switch and flicked it up, then down. Nothing happened.

"Do you think someone tripped the main breaker?" Nancy asked.

"Probably."

Moving swiftly in the dark, Nancy went down the narrow aisle and shone the light into the first cubicle. There was a desk topped with a computer. A tall file cabinet and printer sat next to the desk.

"This has to be where the reporters work," Nancy said as she rushed to the next cubicle. "Maybe Brenda's in one of them."

They checked the offices on both sides of the aisle, but there was no sign of Brenda.

Then Nancy heard another moan. "What's that?"

Ned spun in the direction of the noise. An open door beyond the large room led to a small, dark office.

Nancy beamed the light into the room. Brenda was sprawled facedown on a large, wooden desk. Blood matted the back of her hair.

Ned bent and felt the pulse on Brenda's wrist. "Her pulse is strong. But she's unconscious. I'll call Nine-one-one."

He stood up and reached for the phone. Nancy started for the office door. "I'll be right back," she told Ned. "Whoever did this to Brenda might still be in the building—and I want to find him!"

"Boy, Hannah Gruen can cook as well as Aunt Gertrude," Joe said, patting his full stomach. He was stretched out on the sofa in the squad lounge. The lounge had several comfortable chairs and a coffee table covered with magazines. Messages, crew names, schedules, and a calendar were tacked on a large bulletin board.

Joe used the remote control to turn off the TV. The six o'clock news had just ended.

He and Frank were alone. Luke and Jessica had left on a run, transporting a nursing home patient to and from the hospital.

"Don't tell Aunt Gertrude that," Frank warned. "She likes to think she's the world's best cook." He stood by the communications center. It housed a scanner, two speakers, a phone, and a pager unit that went to a central emergency operations center—EOC. If the emergency call was for the River Heights Rescue Squad, the dispatcher at the EOC triggered a tone that rang through the squad building and the squad's communications center. Individual EMTs' pagers, walkie-talkies, and scanners as well as the ambulance radios also received the signal.

The tone was followed by a message from the 911 dispatcher, stating where and what the emergency was.

But just then, things were quiet except for the "traffic"—the talk and information continually coming in over the scanner. Frank was flipping through the logbook, hunting for the two nights when the body snatchings had taken place.

"Find anything interesting?" Joe asked.

"Nothing we don't already know," Frank said. "Mike and Renee took the call both nights the bodies were snatched. Coincidence or did they plan it?"

Joe shrugged. "Now that we know how the crews work, it could just be coincidence. Especially if Luke and Jessica were already out on a call."

"They were," Frank noted.

"I think we need to talk to Mike and Renee," Joe said.

"We need to talk to all the EMTs, including the day crew," Frank said. "Remember, they can all monitor the night calls with their walkie-talkies and pagers. Anyone interested in dead bodies can tune in when the tones ring on their pagers. So anyone connected with the squad could be in on the body snatching."

Joe folded his arms over his chest. "So how are we going to question everybody without arousing suspicion?"

"Maybe we need to hang around the squad during the day," Frank said as he shut the logbook. "Luke said that since Mike and Renee are out of a job, they've been volunteering for the day crew."

Joe gave a harsh laugh. "I don't think Mike and Renee are going to want to be friendly with the two guys who took their jobs. Besides," he added, "when are we going to sleep?"

Frank laughed. "Maybe tonight will be quiet."

"Rescue Five, possible head injury, female, *Times* newspaper office, One-twelve Main Street," the EOC dispatcher announced over the loudspeaker.

Joe and Frank exchanged horrified glances.

"That's where Pam Harter worked," Joe said.

"And the girl who passed out the other day, Brenda, works there, too," Frank added.

They leapt into action, running the length of the hall and down the steps to the ambulance bays. Unit No. 53 was waiting and ready.

Joe pressed the garage door opener, and Frank jumped in the driver's side and started the engine.

"Let's just hope Nancy's all right!" Frank said, his heart racing.

Brenda's attacker has got to be here, Nancy thought as she crept through a second dark office. Her penlight beam reflected off computer screens.

Who could it be? Nancy wondered. And what did he or she want from Brenda?

Nancy froze at the sound of muffled footsteps. Instantly she flicked off her flashlight and hunched down beside a tall file cabinet. Holding her breath, she listened.

Another footstep. Then the creak of door hinges. Nancy turned in the direction of the sounds. They came from the hall outside the office where she was hiding.

A door softly clicked shut.

Crouching down, Nancy headed for the hall. This is stupid, she told herself. Wait for help.

Only by the time help arrived, it might be too late. Brenda's attacker would get away.

Cautiously, Nancy straightened and crept into

the hall. To the left was a heavy, metal, outside-exit door. Nancy didn't think the intruder had gone that way. The door would have made too much noise.

She glanced to her right. There was one other door. Inch by inch she reached for the doorknob, grasped it, and slowly turned. The door swung open.

The room inside was pitch black. Nancy smelled the musty scent of old papers. She figured she was in a storage room. She blinked, trying to adjust her eyes to the darkness. Tall towers of white loomed in front of her. Stepping inside the room, she reached out and touched one of the towers. They were bundles of old newspapers, stacked high.

Again she held her breath and listened. The room was silent. But the noise had come from here. The intruder *had* to be in the room, hiding somewhere.

Suddenly a tremor of fear ran through Nancy. Her instinct told her to get out and call for help. Slowly she started to back out. Then she looked up and saw two of the towers of paper swaying gently. Suddenly, without a sound, they toppled forward—plunging right at her head!

Chapter Seven

NANCY SCREAMED. Raising both arms, she shielded her face. The heavy papers crashed on top of her, knocking her to the concrete floor.

Nancy struggled, but the bundled stacks felt like concrete blocks. Their weight pinned her arms to her chest and pressed her body against the floor. She couldn't move!

Dust and dirt clogged her nostrils. Nancy screamed for help, but the suffocating papers muffled the sound.

Then she heard a faint voice. Someone was calling her name.

"In here!" she cried, but it came out in a rasping cough.

"Nancy!" the voice was louder.

Taking a deep breath, Nancy thrust her arms

forward with all her might, hoping to dislodge the papers crushing her chest.

"Nancy, are you under there?" someone called above her. Then she heard a thud, followed by another. The weight on her chest felt lighter, and she could breathe. Seconds later a third stack was pulled off, and she could just make out Ned's anxious face peering down at her. He briefly flashed a light down at her, making her blink.

"What happened?" he asked as he yanked away two more stacks of papers. Nancy coughed, then struggled onto her elbows. Her legs were still pinned under an avalanche of newspapers.

She shook her head. "I'm not sure." While Ned pulled off the rest of the bundles, Nancy told him what had happened. "Did you see anyone leaving the area? When the papers fell on top of me, I couldn't see or hear a thing."

He shook his head. "No. But when I was searching for you, I heard a clunk. Someone could have escaped through the exit door."

Ned pulled the last of the stacks off Nancy's legs, then helped her to her feet. Wrapping his arms around her shoulders, he held her close.

Suddenly several lights in the building flicked on. Stepping back, Nancy looked into the hall. "Who did that? And how's Brenda?" she asked quickly.

"I think she's okay. She came to before the Hardys arrived. As soon as they started checking her over, she started giving them orders."

"Joe and Frank are here?"

Ned nodded. "When they came, I borrowed a flashlight and went to look for you. Brenda must have told them where the electric panel was."

Nancy found the storage room light switch and flipped it on. Then she climbed over a bundle of papers to look behind the remaining, still-standing towers. There was about a foot-wide space between the back wall and the papers.

"The intruder must have squeezed in here," Nancy said. "When I came in, he shoved the paper towers with enough force that some of them toppled over."

"He?" Ned asked.

Nancy made her way back to the doorway. "Or she. What did Brenda say? Did she see who hit her?"

"I didn't get a chance to ask. I was too worried about you." Ned squeezed Nancy's hand. "Are you sure you're okay?"

"I'm fine." Walking briskly into the hall, Nancy checked the exit door. Since it was a fire exit, it wasn't locked from the inside. "You're probably right—our mysterious person escaped through here." She opened the door and peered outside. She saw a dark, empty alley. "Whoever it was disappeared in a hurry. Let's go ask Brenda if she has any clues about who attacked her—and why."

When they approached Brenda, Nancy could hear her protesting shrilly.

"No, I'm fine. It's just a small—ouch! That hurts!"

"You'll have to go to the hospital," Frank was saying when Ned and Nancy came into the small office. "This may need stitches."

"Nancy!" Brenda was sitting in the chair behind the desk, holding up her hair. Frank gently pressed a four-by-four pad on the back of her neck while Joe checked her blood pressure.

"Did you catch the creep who hit me?" Brenda asked. Her face was pale. Nancy hoped she was okay.

Nancy shook her head.

"He almost got Nancy," Ned said. He quickly told everyone how he'd found her buried under an avalanche of papers.

"What's going on?" Joe asked as he put away the blood pressure cuff. "First we find you three at the scene of a murder, then at the scene of an assault."

"That's what I'd like to know," Nancy said seriously. "Brenda, why would someone knock you out? Is anything missing? Should we call the police?"

"I've already called my father," Brenda said. Frowning, she leaned forward and checked a pile of papers on the desk. "And no, oddly enough, nothing's missing."

"What were you doing?" Ned asked.

Brenda waved to the files spread out on the desk. "Looking through Pam's folders, hoping to find anything on the story she was working on before she was killed. Pam stored a lot of stuff on the computer, but she also kept notes and copies of articles and interviews in these folders."

"So you didn't see or hear whoever came in?" Nancy asked.

Brenda sighed. "No. I was bending down, pulling folders out of the desk drawer when the lights went out. Two seconds later I heard a footstep. I jerked upright, then *whap.*"

Nancy exchanged glances with Ned.

"Then it must have been two people," she said.

"Right," Frank agreed. "One to turn out the lights."

"And one to hit me!" Brenda said angrily.

Nancy thought a second. "Okay, so the intruders didn't take anything. But they obviously wanted something from Pam's files—what?"

Brenda arched an eyebrow. "I know what they wanted. Luckily, they didn't get it."

Nancy's eyes widened. "What?"

"This." Brenda held up a manila folder on the desk. "When I got conked on the head, I slumped on top of this folder so they couldn't see it."

Frank, Joe, Ned, and Nancy's gazes all went from Brenda to the folder in front of her.

"That's information about the big story Pam was working on?" Nancy asked.

Brenda nodded. "Yup. And guess who Pam was investigating?"

"Blaine Young?" Ned suggested.

"I wish it were Blaine, but no, the file isn't on that conceited playboy." Pausing, Brenda waved the folder dramatically in the air. "The information in the file is on our own state representative —Margaret Cavallo!"

Chapter Eight

MARGARET CAVALLO! Frank thought, his mind racing. It was her half brother's body that had recently been stolen. She was the one breathing down Captain Graham's and Chief McGinnis's necks about the body snatching case. Was there some strange connection?

Glancing up, he caught Nancy's eye. She was biting her lip and frowning. She'd obviously made the connection, too. It could be just a coincidence, Frank thought, although he had learned that when a person's name popped up twice, it usually meant something important.

Frank reached over Brenda's shoulder for the file. "May I see this?" he asked.

She eyed him suspiciously, and Frank realized he'd made a mistake. Frank Hardy, EMT, wouldn't be interested in Pam Harter's files. He was going to have to watch his step around Brenda.

"So are you two taking Brenda to the hospital?" Nancy asked quickly, her gaze darting to Frank.

"Yes," Joe said just as quickly. Standing up, he bustled around, gathering equipment. Frank picked up a roll of gauze and a fresh pad. Holding the pad to the wound, he began to wrap the gauze around Brenda's head.

"Hey!" she protested. "That's going to look stupid."

"No, it's going to look like a turban," Frank said, trying to be patient.

Just then Brenda's father, Frazier Carlton, stormed into the small office.

"What's going on!" he demanded. "What's this about an intruder?" When he saw the white gauze, his face paled. "Brenda? You didn't tell me you'd been hurt. Are you all right, honey?"

The older man rushed to her side. Brenda smiled wanly. "I think so, Daddy," she said. "It was just so horrible."

Frank rolled his eyes. Two seconds ago she'd been bossing everyone around.

"Your daughter needs to go to the hospital and get the wound looked at," Joe said in an official voice.

Frazier nodded. "I'll take her myself."

"We don't recommend that," Joe said.

"I'll sign a release form if I have to," Mr.

Carlton stated abruptly, then he turned his attention back to Brenda. "Now tell me what happened."

While Brenda was talking, Frank secured the gauze, then pulled Nancy out of the office.

"What do you think about Margaret Cavallo, Nan?" he asked in a low voice.

Nancy glanced over her shoulder. "I need to get a look at that file before I decide anything. Which may not be easy if Brenda decides this is her exclusive case."

Ned came up, his hands jammed in his jacket pockets. "Is this a private meeting?" he asked.

"No." Nancy slipped her arm through his. "Frank and I both agree that Margaret Cavallo may be worth investigating."

"Wait a minute. Are you suggesting our state representative might be hiding something?"

"We're not suggesting anything yet," Frank said. "But it *was* her half brother's body that disappeared from that ambulance. What do you know about Sam Cavallo, Nancy?"

"The only thing I've heard was that he was a colorful character who liked to gamble," Nancy said. "But that was just gossip. There was never anything in the papers."

"Probably because Margaret Cavallo was able to keep it out," Frank said.

Ned frowned. "No way. I'm a fan of Ms. Cavallo. She's been a super representative and totally honest. I think you guys are way off base."

"Maybe," Nancy said. "But we all know she's

considering running for governor. What if her half brother's reputation got in the way of her political ambitions? What if she 'arranged' a car accident to get him out of the way?"

Frank snapped his fingers. "Right! She could have had someone slip him a tranquilizer that night. Then when he drove home, he had a convenient accident."

"And to make sure an autopsy didn't show anything suspicious, she had his body stolen," Nancy added.

"What?" Ned cut in. "Are you two saying Ms. Cavallo had her half brother bumped off, then stole his body? That's crazy!" He shot both of them a look of disbelief, then stormed off.

Frank glanced at Nancy. "He's right. It *is* far-fetched, but then a lot of crimes don't make sense."

"And right now, it's the only lead we've got—on either case," Nancy said. "Except for what Ned and I discovered about Blaine Young."

Frank gave a frustrated sigh. "And that doesn't help Joe and me. So if Princess Brenda does let you see what's in the file on Margaret Cavallo, you let me know if there's *anything* that might shed light on our case."

"Right. If there is anything interesting, I may just pay Ms. Cavallo a call tomorrow," Nancy said.

"And Joe and I can ask Chief McGinnis for the police report on Sam's accident."

"Good. Then let's meet for an early dinner

tomorrow night—before your shift," Nancy said. "I'll make sure nosy Brenda doesn't come, so we can speak freely. If we work together, we should be able to solve both cases in no time!"

An hour later Frank was back at the squad building in the men's shower, hot water streaming over his body as he rinsed off the soap. Tilting his head, he let the sharp spray beat against his face.

When they'd returned, the two Hardys had restocked the ambulance. Tonight Joe was completing the call sheet on Brenda. Luke and Jessica had left on a run.

Frank turned off the shower and dried himself. Then he wrapped the towel around his waist, tucked in a corner to secure it, and stepped onto the cool tile. He looked at his watch propped on the narrow counter over the sink. Ten o'clock. Maybe the rest of the shift would be quiet.

Frank checked out his wet hair in the foggy mirror. A noise from the adjoining room made him pause. Turning, he glanced out the doorway leading to the men's locker room. The steam made it hard to see. Was someone out there?

Luke couldn't be back from his run already, so it must be Joe, Frank figured.

He finished finger-combing his hair, then peered around the locker room door. Someone was stooped over, rooting through Joe's locker. Frank could just see the person's back.

"Joe? Did you finish that report already?"

The person froze. Frank frowned and, sticking his head farther into the room, looked closer. Long, black hair cascaded from beneath a baseball cap.

Definitely not Joe.

"Excuse me," Frank said, "but what are you doing snooping in my brother's locker?"

Startled, the person jumped up. Frank realized it was a girl, even though she had her back to him. Quick as a deer, she dove for the doorknob.

"Hey!" Frank grabbed his towel and ran after her. He reached for her arm just as she opened the door.

Without turning, she struck out, catching him on the chin. Surprised by the sharp blow, Frank jerked backward. His feet slipped on the tile, and with a cry, he lost his balance, and fell heavily to the floor.

"Hey!"

Frank's cry echoed through the squad building. Reacting instinctively, Joe dropped his pen and ran through the lounge. He looked down the hall and saw someone racing toward the door leading to the garage. Even though the person wore a long raincoat and had a baseball cap pulled over black hair, Joe could tell it was a girl.

Joe took off after her. He didn't know who she was or what she wanted, but he was going to find out.

"Stop!" Joe called out. Flinging the door open, the girl disappeared.

Joe heard her footsteps pounding down the

stairs. If she made it to the garage, she'd escape! He yanked the door open and took the stairs two at a time.

She was racing for the outside door when Joe cried out another warning. She didn't slow down for even an instant.

Gritting his teeth, Joe tackled the girl around the waist. She screamed as they crashed to the floor. The baseball cap flew off.

She lashed out, catching Joe in the cheek. Angry, he grabbed her shoulders and flipped her onto her back. Her long, dark hair covered her face, but Joe brushed it aside.

Instantly he recognized her. It was Renee Torres, the EMT who had been on the night squad. She glared at him, her eyes snapping.

"Let me go," she spat. Pulling her arms from his grasp, she tried to push him off.

"Hey!" Joe caught her wrists. Something was in her right hand.

Joe jerked the hand closer to see what it was. His eyes widened.

It was his wallet.

Renee Torres had stolen his wallet!

Chapter Nine

"WHAT ARE YOU DOING with my wallet?" Joe demanded.

"Nothing!" Renee snapped. For a second she stopped struggling.

"Nothing?" Joe frowned down at her. Her eyes were dark with long lashes and black brows. Her lips were rosy and full, even when pressed together in an angry line. He'd met Renee only briefly when the day crew had been introduced by Captain Graham. But he hadn't forgotten how gorgeous she was.

A thumping down the stairs told Joe that Frank had arrived.

"Are you all right, Frank?" Joe asked. "I heard you holler." Without releasing Renee, he glanced up. He bit back a grin when he saw that Frank was wearing only a towel.

"Yeah, but I'd sure like to know—" Frank stopped in midsentence when he saw who Joe was holding. "Renee Torres? What's going on? Why were you snooping in Joe's locker?"

"That's what *I'd* like to know," Joe said, looking back down. "She had my wallet. I left it in there by mistake when we went on our run to the *Times*. Even though Frank was driving, I should have had my license on me."

Renee frowned and tilted her head sideways. "The whole thing was a stupid idea."

"What was?" Joe asked, but the loud *brum, brum* of the tones cut him off.

"Rescue Five, four-vehicle accident northbound lane Interstate fifty-five, mile marker two-two-four" blasted over the loudspeaker system.

"That sounds bad," Frank said. "I've got to get some clothes on." Spinning on his bare feet, he thudded back up the stairs.

For a second Joe and Renee stared at each other. Joe didn't want to let her go without an explanation, but he had to respond immediately.

"Let me go with you," Renee said. "A four-vehicle accident will need all our help. Especially since you two aren't experienced," she added sharply.

Joe hesitated, then said, "All right. But as soon as it's over, I want to know why you had my wallet." Letting go of Renee's wrist, he plucked his wallet from her fingers. Then he stood up and extended his hand to help her up. Ignoring it, she jumped to her feet and headed for the row of coats hanging on pegs. They were made of heavy, waterproof material and had bright, reflective stripes on them.

Ten minutes later Frank drove the crash truck, the vehicle used for car accidents, down the interstate. Since it was late, traffic was light. But the earlier rain and falling temperature made the road slick.

Renee sat in the back of the truck, her rescue helmet on her lap, staring straight ahead. Joe could see her silhouette through the pass-through. He couldn't help but wonder what she'd been doing in his locker. Why had she taken his wallet? He didn't think she was the intruder he'd surprised the other night in the ambulance. She was too small.

Turning around in his seat, Joe tried to push Renee from his mind. They were almost to the 224-mile marker. He could see flashing lights ahead. Flares were set out in the passing lane. From his EMT training, he knew how complicated a vehicle rescue could be.

A jumble of cars, trucks, and two police cars were on the median strip. A car and a pickup truck were badly damaged, a third car had a smashed rear, and a tractor trailer had flipped onto its side.

Joe spotted Unit No. 51. Luke and Jessica must have heard the call over their radio. The two EMTs were huddled around the overturned tractor. A police officer was helping them extricate the driver.

As soon as Frank pulled the ambulance safely off the highway, Joe grabbed his primary bag and helmet and climbed from the crash truck. Renee was already striding toward a woman holding two screaming children. Her helmet was on and her primary bag was clutched in her hand. A police officer knelt by the older child. Blood streamed from the child's forehead.

Frank and Joe hurried to the tractor trailer. "Do you need help, Luke?" Joe called.

"Check the other vehicles," Luke said.

Joe and Frank hurried to the nearest car. The driver, an older man, sat in the driver's seat, staring through the windshield in a daze.

"I'll take care of him," Frank said over his shoulder. "You check out the pickup."

The shiny, new pickup appeared to have been totaled. As Joe jogged toward it, he had a sinking feeling in the pit of his stomach. A groan from inside told him someone was still in the truck. When he peered through the smashed passenger window, he saw two guys about his age. Both were conscious. The driver held his forehead.

"I think I'm okay," the passenger said weakly. "Check my buddy out."

Joe smelled beer on his breath. "Don't move before I can look you over," he told the guy before running around to the driver's side.

By the time Joe had the two teens patched up, a

small group of spectators had formed. A lone police officer was attempting to keep them away. One spectator, a tall man with long, stringy hair, broke away from the group and came over to Ambulance No. 51. Luke and Jessica were bent over the truck driver, who was lying on the wheeled stretcher.

As the tall guy strode over, Luke jumped up. Grabbing the guy's elbow, Luke steered him away from the ambulance. Joe knew from his training that spectators could be a nuisance, so he hurried over.

"Need help?" he asked.

Luke shook his head. Joe directed his attention to the tall guy, who wore an army-type jacket and boots. A light growth of whiskers made his chin look dirty.

"Look, Freddie," Luke said, his tone sharp, "if you want to help, keep the crowd away from the accident before someone else gets hurt."

"Okay, okay." The guy named Freddie bobbed his head eagerly. Turning, he spread out his arms and in an authoritative voice started shouting, "Keep back please! Keep back!"

Luke blew out his breath. "Accidents are hard enough without guys like that around."

"What do you mean?" Joe asked.

"Oh, there are always ambulance chasers. And I don't mean lawyers looking for clients or nosy people who naturally stop to watch. I mean people who get their kicks from being at the scene of an accident, you know?"

Joe didn't. "That sounds kind of sick. Is that Freddie guy one of them?"

"Yeah. The EMTs call him First There Freddie because sometimes he's at an accident scene even before the rescue crews get there."

Joe's brows shot up. "He is? But how does he know about the calls?"

Luke shrugged as he started back toward Unit No. 51. "Who knows."

"Wow." For a second Joe thought about the information. Maybe First There Freddie wasn't just an ambulance chaser. Maybe he was scouting out accidents for another reason—such as checking to see if there were any dead victims.

The idea gave Joe goose bumps.

"Luke," Joe called as he caught up to him, "was Freddie around the nights the bodies were stolen?"

"I think I remember Renee mentioning something about Freddie being around for the last one. But you'd better ask her."

Don't worry, I will, Joe thought. Especially since I have a few other questions, too. He also decided to keep his eye on Freddie and get the license number of the vehicle he was driving.

"Joe!" Frank waved him over to the car with the older man. A cervical collar was around the man's neck, and an inflatable splint circled his wrist.

"We need to transport Mr. Anderson to the hospital," Frank said. Together the Hardys lifted the man from the car and placed him onto the stretcher. Frank covered him with a blanket, then they secured him with straps and carried the stretcher to the ambulance.

After sliding the stretcher into the patient compartment, Frank climbed in to prepare Mr. Anderson for transport.

"Before we leave, I'm going to see if Renee needs help," Joe said to his brother. The last time he'd seen her, she'd been leading the woman and her children over to Ambulance No. 51.

"Don't be too long," Frank said.

Joe crossed the damp grass. By now the place was swarming with rescue personnel, police officers, and firefighters. For a second he scanned the area, searching for Freddie. He saw the guy loping across the highway to a pickup parked along the side.

As the pickup pulled away, Joe memorized the license. "Gotcha," he said under his breath. Later he and Frank could check Freddie out.

When he reached Unit No. 51, he hunted for Renee. The woman she'd been caring for was sitting on a blanket. Her two kids were asleep, their heads in her lap. A police officer was asking the woman questions about the accident.

"Did you see Renee?" Joe asked Jessica. She was putting supplies back into her primary bag.

Jessica shook her head.

Where could she have gone? Joe wondered.

Pulling off his helmet, he looked around. A big, burly guy with a mustache was looking back at him. He stood by a car parked in the median strip about fifty yards ahead of the ambulance.

For a second Joe didn't recognize him. Then he realized who it was—Mike Hosford, the EMT who worked with Renee.

Joe waved his hand. "Hey!" he called as he jogged across the grass.

Hosford shot him a nasty look, then yanked open his car door and jumped in. With a spray of mud, the car sped off.

Joe stopped. In the light of the flares and flashing strobes, he caught a glimpse of a second person in the car with Mike.

A girl with long, black hair.

Renee Torres.

Chapter Ten

"RENEE SURE DID a disappearing act," Joe said an hour later. The two Hardys were sipping cups of hot chocolate from the hospital vending machine.

Mr. Anderson had been delivered to the hospital emergency room. Frank was filling out the pre–hospital patient care report. Joe had met and talked with Mrs. Anderson, who had been contacted by the nurse. Now the Hardys were waiting for the okay from the emergency room staff to leave.

"I never got to ask her why she took my wallet," Joe added.

Frank glanced up from the two-page form. "It is strange that she took off so fast, especially since there was lots to do at the scene and she volunteered to help. What do you think she's hiding?"

"I don't know, but Mike Hosford sure gave me a deadly look when he took off with her." Joe swallowed the last of his hot chocolate, then crumpled the paper cup and tossed it into a trash bin.

"Well, at least now we have some definite suspects to check out besides Margaret Cavallo," Frank said as he skimmed the completed form.

"Don't forget that Freddie guy," Joe reminded his brother. "We need to call McGinnis with that license plate number to see if Freddie has a real name and any kind of record."

"Yeah. We might just crack this case yet." Frank suddenly yawned. "That is, if we can stay awake long enough to investigate!"

"Let me do the talking," Nancy whispered to Brenda as they walked up the stairs to Margaret Cavallo's office. The representative had a suite on the third floor of a renovated building in downtown River Heights.

Brenda halted and her brows shot up. Nancy could see a small bandage peeking from beneath her ponytail. "Why should I let you do all the talking?" Brenda declared. "I found the file."

Nancy sighed. "Because I've had tons of experience interviewing people. And we need to be careful. If we tip Ms. Cavallo off, she'll clam up about her brother. Then we'll never know if she's guilty of playing a part in his death."

"Oh, she's guilty all right." Brenda snorted as she started back up the steps. "And she's guilty of killing Pam, too. That file of Pam's proved it."

"It proved nothing," Nancy protested. "Pam just had clippings of everything that related to Sam Cavallo's death, the disappearance of his body as well as Ms. Cavallo's career."

"That's proof enough for me," Brenda said as she reached the landing. "Pam was investigating Ms. Cavallo. I'll bet she found lots of dirt on our wonderful state representative."

"But we didn't find anything like that in Pam's file," Nancy protested.

Brenda waved her hand. "Pam's probably got them on a computer disk. Or maybe those creeps last night did steal some information. Anyway, when Margaret Cavallo found out Pam was snooping around, she had Pam killed."

"Brenda!" Nancy exclaimed. "That's a wild guess. If you say anything like that to Ms. Cavallo—"

"Don't worry, I won't!" Brenda cut Nancy off. Turning, she faced Nancy. "Just remember—*I'm* the reporter here, and this is *my* story. I know how to get information out of our sly Ms. Cavallo." With those words, Brenda spun around and marched down the carpeted hall.

Nancy took a deep breath. This was going to be a disaster.

Ten minutes later, the two girls sat on a modern sofa in the waiting area. Brenda had called earlier, requesting an interview for *Today's*

Times. When the two girls arrived, the receptionist had asked them to take a seat.

The interview idea was a great way to find out some things about the representative. Nancy just hoped when they did meet Margaret Cavallo, Brenda wouldn't blow it.

"So what were you and Frank Hardy whispering about last night?" Brenda's question broke into Nancy's thoughts.

"What?" Nancy turned and looked at her.

"Frank Hardy," Brenda repeated. "You two were awfully chummy last night. I saw you talking outside the office. Are you sure all he did was teach you CPR? I mean, he is *really* cute," she added.

Picking up a magazine, Nancy tried to ignore Brenda's nosy questions. "Like I said, he taught a course I took, and that's it."

"Yeah, sure," Brenda said.

"Ms. Carlton? Ms. Drew?" The receptionist stood up. "Ms. Cavallo will meet with you now."

Grateful for the interruption, Nancy rose and crossed the carpeted floor. The receptionist opened the door and ushered them in.

Margaret Cavallo was talking on the phone. She waved for Nancy and Brenda to sit down on two chairs pulled up in front of the desk.

While Ms. Cavallo finished her conversation, Nancy studied her. The attractive woman was in her late forties. She wore a navy blue suit and a crisp white blouse. Her only jewelry was a gold bracelet. Her sleek, gray-streaked, brown hair was pulled back in a loose bun. Nancy thought the representative looked both feminine and professional.

"So you two ladies are here to interview me," Ms. Cavallo said when she hung up.

"Yes," Brenda replied, not bothering to introduce Nancy. "My father, Frazier Carlton, owns *Today's Times.* I'm on the staff."

Ms. Cavallo smiled. "Yes. I know your father well. *Today's Times* was very supportive during my campaign." She smiled politely. "Now, what can I help you with? Are you interested in my views on any recent legislation? Or—"

"What we really want to know about is the death of your half brother," Brenda said, jumping in before Nancy even had a chance to say anything. "Are you secretly glad he's not around anymore to mess up your future plans to run for governor?"

Nancy's mouth fell open. She couldn't believe even Brenda would be stupid enough to ask her a question like that.

Ms. Cavallo's smile faded. "Excuse me?" she asked, her voice icy.

"That's not what Brenda meant, Ms. Cavallo," Nancy said quickly. She shot an angry look at Brenda. "We're covering the recent ambulance hijackings. We thought you might know of anyone who might want—"

Abruptly Margaret Cavallo stood up. A scowl had replaced her polite smile. "No. I think Ms. Carlton does want to know all about my relationship with my half brother. Only that's none of the public's business. Now, if you'll excuse me, I have work to do."

Brenda jumped up. "But what about the fact that Pam Harter had a fat file on you?"

"Brenda! Shut up," Nancy muttered between clenched teeth. Standing, she grabbed Brenda's arm and dragged her toward the door.

"And now Pam's *dead,"* Brenda continued as she jerked her arm from Nancy's grasp. "How do you explain that?"

Ms. Cavallo pressed the buzzer on her desk. Immediately the receptionist appeared.

"Escort these two *reporters* from my office," she ordered.

"I knew you were hiding something," Brenda declared as Nancy pushed her out of the office. "I'll tell my father that you threw us out!"

When they were in the hall, the receptionist slammed the door behind them.

"Real smooth, Brenda," Nancy said.

"Yeah, but we got what we wanted." Spinning around, Brenda marched down the hallway. "Did you see the guilt written all over Cavallo's face when I mentioned her wanting to get rid of her half brother?"

Nancy rolled her eyes. "No, I didn't. Besides, you can't arrest a person because she looks guilty. And now she's so furious, she'll never talk to us."

Brenda stopped on the top of the stairs. "She was pretty mad, wasn't she?"

Nancy nodded. "So mad, she'll probably call your father and chew him out."

Brenda shrugged. "Oh, who cares about that. I'm worried about her thugs."

"What thugs?"

"The ones who attacked me last night," Brenda said. "What if she sends them after us?"

"We don't know who they were, much less that they were *her* thugs," Nancy said as she started down the steps.

"True," Brenda said. Nervously she glanced over her shoulder. "Still, I don't want another whack on the head."

"You should've thought of that before you shot your big mouth off." Nancy strode through the lobby and out the front door.

"I was asking probing questions," Brenda shot back. She had to jog to keep up with Nancy, who walked briskly down the sidewalk. "Where are you going?"

"To find Blaine Young."

"Blaine? But I told you, Pam didn't even have a file on Blaine."

"I know." Nancy stopped at her Mustang. "And the police checked out his alibi. Several people at Winters saw him that night. Still, the medical examiner said Pam was killed between six and seven. That means he could have murdered her, then gone to Winters."

Brenda's brows shot up. "He sounds pretty guilty, huh?"

"I don't know. But maybe I'll get an idea after I talk with him."

"I'm coming with you." Brenda started to open the passenger door.

"Oh, no, you're not," Nancy declared. "Not after that performance in Ms. Cavallo's office."

Brenda put her hands on her hips. "Oh, come on, Nancy. I promise I'll let you do all the talking this time. Besides, you don't even know Blaine. I can call his office and find out where he's working today."

Nancy hesitated. The last person she wanted along was Brenda Carlton. Only Brenda was right. Nancy had never even met Blaine, so it was doubtful he'd talk to her.

Nancy sighed. "All right. But not one word!"

An hour later Nancy and Brenda rode a noisy elevator up to the top floor of River Heights's newest skyscraper. Both girls wore hard hats. The field manager on the ground floor had let them go up only when Nancy told them they were friends from out of town who'd arrived to help the "grieving" Blaine recover from the death of his girlfriend.

"Do you think this thing will fall?" Brenda asked worriedly. The elevator walls were enclosed, so they couldn't see out.

"Let's hope not," Nancy said. Just then the elevator screeched and banged to a halt. When the doors opened, Nancy stepped out. The floor of the new building was constructed of concrete, but there were no walls. She could see all the way to the Muskoka River.

Nancy gulped. "Uh, we're here."

Behind her, Brenda gasped. "Oh, my gosh—all I see is sky! Where are the walls?"

"Look, there's Blaine." Nancy pointed to the left. Two guys in hard hats were staring at a set of plans they held between them. As the younger man talked, he gestured right, then left.

Picking her way over piles of lumber and supplies, Nancy walked toward them.

"Hey, wait for me!" Brenda called. When she caught up to Nancy, she grabbed her arm. "We're a long way up. Do you think this place is safe?"

"No," Nancy said, then turned her attention to Blaine Young, whom she recognized from the photo. He was medium tall with broad shoulders. He wore khaki-colored slacks and a blue button-down shirt with a tie loosened at the knot. As Nancy approached, he stopped talking and frowned at her.

"Who are you?" he asked brusquely. "When Charlie called up he said I knew you two girls. That you were here for a surprise visit."

"We are here for a surprise visit, Mr. Young," Nancy said smoothly. "We'd like to ask you some questions about Pam Harter."

Blaine's eyes narrowed. Turning to the other man, he said, "Excuse me, Harry. This will only take a minute." He handed Harry the plans, then roughly took Nancy's arm and steered her out of earshot. Brenda followed, glancing down nervously as they moved closer to the building's edge.

"What do you mean—questions about Pam?" Blaine demanded. "Who are you two?" He glanced from Nancy to Brenda. "Wait a minute," he said, sticking his finger in Brenda's face. "Aren't you that nosy reporter from the *Times?"*

"Yes, and I was Pam's friend, too," Brenda replied shortly.

"And I'm Nancy Drew. I'm a detective investigating Pam's murder. I thought you might have an idea—"

"No, I don't," Blaine cut in. "And I don't have anything to say to a snoopy reporter and nosy detective, either. So you two girls get out of here. It's not safe."

"Oh, you were eager to have us come up when you thought we were girlfriends from out of town," Brenda taunted. "I guess you must really miss Pam."

Blaine scowled. "My feelings for Pam are none of your business."

"We know that, Mr. Young," Nancy said calmly. If only she could get a few answers before Brenda ruined this interview, too. "We're concerned—"

"Oh, but your feelings are important," Brenda cut in. "Motive, remember? You must have really hated it when Pam started investigating *you."*

Blaine looked as surprised as Nancy.

"That's crazy!" he snapped. Raising a finger,

he poked Brenda in the shoulder. "And if I were you, I'd quit throwing around false accusations and get out of here. Before I do something I regret!"

Nancy watched as Brenda's face turned white and her eyes grew wide with fright. Nervously she stepped backward.

"Brenda, let's go," Nancy said quickly. All of a sudden, she had a bad feeling. They were up too high, and when she glanced behind her, she noticed Harry had disappeared.

Brenda nodded. Keeping her eyes on Blaine, she tried to get around him. One high heel caught on an electric cord and she lost her balance.

Blaine reached out. Instinctively, Brenda jerked away from him. Throwing her arms wide, she screamed as she fell backward.

Nancy gasped. Brenda was only a foot away from the edge of the building. If she fell over the side, she'd plunge to her death!

Chapter Eleven

BRENDA!" Nancy screamed as Brenda toppled backward toward blue sky. Dropping her purse, Nancy lunged for the reporter and grabbed her left arm.

Brenda fell against an upright beam, bounced off, and continued to fall sideways. Her mouth was open wide in a silent scream.

Nancy tugged hard, the same instant Blaine dove for Brenda's flailing right arm. Together, the two of them pulled Brenda safely onto the concrete floor.

Crying hysterically, Brenda lay in a heap on the floor. Nancy crouched next to her.

"Are you all right?" she asked, her own breath coming in gasps.

Brenda nodded. Then she looked up. Tears gleamed in her eyes as she glared at Blaine Young, who stood looking down at her.

"You tried to kill me!" she screeched.

His mouth fell open. "What? You tripped!" His gaze darted to Nancy. "You saw what happened. I didn't try to kill her."

Brenda scrambled to her feet. Her sleeve was torn, and mascara ran down her cheeks. Nancy had never seen her so angry. "You did, too!" she accused. "Just like you killed Pam because she dug up some dirt on your precious company. Well, that little scare isn't going to stop me from finding out what she discovered and reporting it to the world."

Blaine's eyes narrowed to slits. "That's it. I've had it with you two and your lies. I told you it wasn't safe up here—so get out!" He jerked his thumb toward the elevator.

"Okay, Mr. Young, we'll leave," Nancy said, trying to stay calm. "But if you have nothing to hide, then why are you avoiding our questions?"

"Because you aren't the police. I've answered their questions. Besides, if I did kill Pam, I wouldn't have been stupid enough to leave her body where I work!"

"Maybe," Brenda snapped right back. She'd smoothed her hair and was dabbing under her eyes with a tissue. "But you obviously called her and left that message for her to meet you here."

Blaine snorted. "Oh, really? Maybe you'd better ask the police about that, too."

"We will," Nancy stated before the reporter could respond. "Come on, Brenda."

Brenda shot Blaine one last angry look, then followed Nancy to the elevator. All the way down, the two girls were silent. Nancy was replaying the incident in her mind. Had it been an accident?

Brenda *had* tripped. But when Blaine reached out, was he trying to catch her or give her a little nudge over the side?

Nancy shook her head. No, that would have been stupid. She would have witnessed the whole thing. And he wouldn't dare push her over, too.

Or would he?

Nancy glanced at Brenda. Her face was pale. Still, she didn't seem too shaken. Maybe Brenda was tougher than she looked.

"So what did Blaine mean about checking with the police on the taped message?" Brenda asked, her voice slightly shaky.

The elevator doors clanged open. Nancy sighed with relief when she stepped onto firm ground. "The police can tell if the voice on the tape is his."

"Oh." Brenda sounded disappointed. "And from the way he was talking they already know it wasn't."

Nancy nodded. "Still, I can ask McGinnis." Tilting back her head, she looked up at the top floor. She wondered if Blaine was up there gloating or if their visit had worried him as it had worried Margaret Cavallo.

Nancy dropped her chin and sighed. If Brenda kept shooting her mouth off, half the people in River Heights would want to push her off a cliff.

"I just wish we could get that 'scoop' you keep referring to. So far I haven't seen any evidence that Blaine or his company has done anything wrong," Nancy said when they reached the Mustang.

"Oh, I'll find it," Brenda said. "Before you picked me up at the *Times* this morning, I hunted everywhere in Pam's office." Her face fell. "Though I must admit, I couldn't find anything more on Margaret or Blaine." Suddenly she snapped her fingers. "Hey. We never checked Pam's apartment!"

"I was thinking the same thing." Opening the car door, Nancy slid behind the wheel. Brenda got in at the same time. "I'm sure the police have checked it from top to bottom, though."

"Yeah, but I remember Pam telling me one of her reporter tricks was keeping information in secret files so no one could steal her scoops," Pam said as she fastened her seat belt.

"She was really into this reporter stuff. But it may just help us solve this case. Do you think Mr. Zeleski will let us in again?" Nancy asked.

"We can always try. And of course if he's not there"—Brenda's eyes twinkled—"we can always break in, right?"

Nancy laughed. "You've been watching too many TV shows," she said. However, if Pam did have important information at her apartment, it just might be worth the chance, Nancy thought.

Twenty minutes later Brenda knocked on Pam's door. When they'd asked the super to let them in, he told them Pam's sister was there so the door would be unlocked.

An attractive woman in her thirties opened the door a crack. Her eyes were red, as if she'd been crying. "Yes?"

"Hi, I'm Brenda Carlton, a reporter for *Today's Times.*"

"I don't want to talk to any more reporters," the woman stated abruptly as she started to shut the door.

Nancy stuck her foot in the crack. "We're not here to ask you questions," she said quickly. "We're investigating Pam's death."

"I'm a friend of Pam's," Brenda added. "We worked together at the paper."

The woman studied them for a second, but didn't open the door.

"You're Pam's sister?" Nancy asked gently. "We were the ones who, um, found her."

Tears filled the woman's eyes. "Oh, that must have been horrible." Opening the door, she stepped back to let them in. "I always told Pam her snooping would get her into trouble. But I never thought she'd . . ." Her voice trailed off, and she dabbed her nose with a wadded-up tissue.

"Did Pam confide in you, Ms., uh—"

"Mrs. Previa. I live in Washington, D.C. I flew

in last night and decided to stay here." She looked around the apartment. "But I'm not sure it was such a good idea."

Brenda touched her on the arm. "My father told me the funeral would be in Washington."

Mrs. Previa nodded. "That's where our family lives."

Nancy glanced around the apartment. It looked as if Pam's sister had packed a few of Pam's personal items.

For a second Mrs. Previa looked puzzled. "Aren't you two a little young to be solving murders?"

"Oh, no." Brenda shook her head earnestly. "We have *years* of experience."

"Oh." Mrs. Previa walked slowly into the kitchen as if in a trance. "Well, I hadn't talked to Pam in ages. She was always busy, and then when she started dating Blaine, she was never here."

"Blaine?" Brenda perked up. "Did she tell you anything about his company, High Designs?"

"No. Mostly she talked about what a great catch he was—ambitious, good-looking." She sighed. "But I don't know . . . Pam had a habit of falling for hotheads."

"Boy, I'll say," Nancy murmured. Then she said, "What about any scoops she was working on for the paper?"

"Pam was very secretive about her work until she broke a story." Mrs. Previa shrugged. "Sorry I can't help you. Now, if you'll excuse me, I need to finish up here."

"If you don't mind we'd like to look through Pam's files," Brenda said.

Mrs. Previa hesitated, then sighed. "I don't suppose Pam would care now," she said sadly.

Nancy and Brenda thanked her and went into Pam's office. Immediately Brenda sat down in the desk chair and began pulling out drawers.

"The police probably took most of that stuff," Nancy said as she started walking slowly around the room. Where would Pam hide information she didn't want anyone else to find? she wondered.

"I know. But maybe she labeled it recipes or something," Brenda said. "Some cop isn't going to figure that's important."

"Maybe." Nancy crouched and peered under the desk. Carefully she ran her fingers across the flat bottom. Nothing.

Standing, Nancy studied the room. If Pam had hidden her files in another part of the apartment, it might take forever to find them.

Nancy's eyes focused on one of the corners. The floor was covered with wall-to-wall carpeting. A straight-backed chair stood against the wall next to the corner. Under it, the rug bulged slightly.

Nancy dropped to her hands and knees. Someone had pulled up the carpet, then retacked it so it would be easy to lift. With her fingertips, Nancy felt a slight ripple under the carpet.

"Find something?" Brenda asked behind her.

"I think so." Carefully Nancy peeled back the edge of carpet. The tacks popped up easily.

A brown clasp envelope peeked from beneath the carpet. "Bingo," Nancy said.

"Quick! Open it!" Brenda said excitedly.

Nancy sat on her heels and undid the clasp. Several papers were inside.

"What do they say?" Brenda prodded.

Standing up, Nancy slid out the papers. Silently she skimmed the top paper. One name leapt out.

Brenda gasped behind her. "I was right! It was Margaret Cavallo."

"Let's finish reading, Brenda, before you jump to conclusions," Nancy said. On the first sheet Pam had jotted down questions about the death of Sam Cavallo: "What happened the night of S. Cavallo's accident? Was M. Cavallo involved? Why won't anyone answer my questions?"

On the second sheet was a log of recent calls Pam had made, mostly to Margaret Cavallo's office. After each call a note was written. Usually it stated "refused to talk," or "refused to see me." The last notation in the log was dated five days earlier.

"Looks like Pam didn't have any luck seeing Cavallo, either," Brenda said.

Nancy nodded. "Yeah." She checked the last phone call on the list. It was to R.H. Diagnostics.

R.H. Diagnostics. Why was it on the list?

Nancy's chin snapped up, and she gripped the page. The medical examiner had found an appointment card for R.H. Diagnostics clutched in Pam's hand. Pam had also noted an appointment on her calendar.

Now here it was again, mentioned in her secret files.

Nancy's mind began to whirl.

Pam might have been at R.H. Diagnostics the same day she was killed. There had to be a connection!

Chapter Twelve

"NANCY, HAVE YOU FLIPPED?" Brenda asked, staring at Nancy as if she were crazy. "What does R.H. Diagnostics have to do with Pam's death?"

"I don't know," Nancy said, pacing across the floor. "But there must be a connection. Why else would Pam have written the phone number in her secret files? Why else would she have been clutching the appointment card when she was murdered?"

Just then Mrs. Previa stuck her head through the doorway. "Did you girls need something else?"

Nancy shook her head. "No. I mean yes. Do you know where Pam's phone book is?"

Mrs. Previa pulled a small leather book from a

desk drawer, then left. Nancy looked up R.H. Diagnostics.

"Are you going to make an appointment, too?" Brenda asked.

"No. I want the address so I can drive over and find out just what R.H. Diagnostics is. Maybe it's a fake business or something that Pam stumbled upon."

Brenda nodded eagerly. "Good. I'll go, too."

"You'd better not. I'm going to call—" Nancy caught herself. She was just about to say that she was going to call the Hardys. They'd want to know about Pam's questions concerning Sam's death. Only she didn't dare say that in front of Brenda.

Brenda frowned suspiciously. "Who were you going to call? Ned? You don't think I'm as good a detective as he is?"

"Yes, Ned," Nancy fibbed quickly. And of course you're not as good as he is, she added to herself. "But I realized he's playing basketball with some friends."

"Oh, good. Then let's go." Brenda headed for the door. "Maybe we can pick up a deli sandwich on the way. I'm starved."

Nancy thanked Mrs. Previa, then asked if it was all right if she took the notes. She was sure Chief McGinnis would want to see them.

Thirty minutes later Nancy drove past R.H. Diagnostics. It was a brick building located on the outskirts of River Heights.

"Judging from the medical symbol on the sign, I'd say R.H. Diagnostics is a clinic," Nancy observed. A half-eaten turkey sandwich lay on the seat beside her. Brenda munched a pastrami sandwich with onions and mustard. The whole car smelled like a deli.

Nancy slowed the Mustang and turned the corner. A small parking lot holding several cars was off to one side. She pulled into one of the slots.

"I'll go in and see if I can figure out what services the clinic offers," she told Brenda as she rewrapped her sandwich and set it on the dashboard.

Nancy quickly got out of the car and entered the building. She paused for a second in the small waiting room. It was tastefully decorated in mauve and gray. Two people flipping through magazines sat in chrome and upholstery chairs. A receptionist worked behind a glass window.

"Excuse me, a friend of mine recommended R.H. Diagnostics," Nancy said. "I wondered if you had any infor—"

Without looking up, the receptionist slid open the glass door and handed Nancy a colorful brochure. "Clinic hours are Monday through Friday, nine to five," she recited in a bored voice. "We're open on Wednesdays and Thursdays until seven."

"Thank you," Nancy said, taking the brochure. She walked briskly out of the building and to the parking lot. When she climbed into the

Mustang, she tossed the brochure on Brenda's lap. "Read that and tell me what you think."

Brenda nodded and opened the brochure. Nancy started the Mustang.

"Well, it sounds like it's a clinic that does complicated tests," Brenda finally said.

"Magnetic resonance imaging for one," Nancy said. "Did Pam mention being sick?"

Brenda shrugged. "Not that I know of. But then she's not the kind of person who would have announced that something was wrong. The clinic takes routine X rays, too," she added. "But I don't remember her breaking any bones, either."

Nancy thought as she headed the car back to the *Times* office to drop Brenda off. She couldn't help but feel disappointed. She'd been so excited when she'd first seen Pam's notes on R.H. Diagnostics. Now she wasn't so sure the place had anything to do with Pam's murder.

"So where are we going?" Brenda asked eagerly. "To track down more clues?"

"No, I'm taking you back to the *Times.*"

"Oh." Brenda sounded disappointed. Nancy had to admit that for the last half an hour Brenda had almost been pleasant company.

"I don't want to go back to the *Times.* Why can't we find out more about Margaret Cavallo or Blaine?" Brenda asked. "And we need to drop those notes off at the police station and ask Chief McGinnis if they checked out this Diagnostics place."

"Whoa, Brenda." Nancy laughed. "I'll stop by

the police department, but then I'm going home because Ned's coming over early for dinner." Which was true, Nancy thought. Only the Hardys were going to be at her house, too, which she didn't dare tell Brenda.

"Oh?" Brenda said, her voice oozing with suspicion. "Is that really what you're going to do? Or are you going to dump me so you can run off and solve this case on your own!"

Nancy sighed. Brenda was back to her old self. She should have known it couldn't last.

"Nice place," Joe said sarcastically as he and Frank tromped up the dark steps of the Oak Terrace Apartments. "Do you think there really is a terrace?"

"Or an oak tree?" Frank chuckled. There was graffiti on the walls of the stairwell, and the whole place smelled like dirty socks.

It was early afternoon. After the Hardys had slept all morning, then eaten a huge brunch of Hannah's ham and eggs, they started working on their case.

Joe stopped on the landing of the third floor. "Well, at least we know one thing about Freddie Bloser, alias First There Freddie. He doesn't live in a posh neighborhood."

"That makes three things we know about the mysterious Freddie," Frank corrected. "We know from McGinnis that he's pumping gas at a local station and that he doesn't have a criminal record."

Joe snorted as he stopped in front of apartment 3C. "Bloser" was written on a piece of paper stuck into the slot under the apartment number. "You mean he doesn't have a criminal record in River Heights. He could be some hired goon from Chicago or New York City."

"Yeah. So what are we going to say if he answers?" Frank asked in a whisper.

"Uh, that we're here to look at a model apartment?" Joe joked. "He's probably not home, since his truck wasn't parked outside. But if he is, we'll apologize for knocking on the wrong door and come back later."

"Well, at least it's a plan." Frank laughed as he rapped on the door. There was no answer.

"Doorbells must cost extra at the Oak Terrace Apartments." Joe knocked harder, then looked at Frank. "Do you want to do the honors of getting in?"

Frank nodded. "Watch the steps. Let me know if anyone's coming."

Five minutes later the Hardys were inside Freddie Bloser's apartment. Joe gave a low whistle.

"Wow. Nice place," he said as he studied the bare floors, peeling paint, and curtainless windows.

Bloser's apartment consisted of a large room with a kitchenette off one end and a bathroom on the other. On Joe's right there was a sagging sofa, a round, plastic-topped table, and two kitchen chairs with the foam stuffing sticking out. To his left there was a dresser and a cot, neatly made.

"Do you think it's for rent—furnished?" Joe quipped.

Frank grimaced. "Let's hope not. I think everything here came from a yard sale." He started walking around. "Let's see if we can find anything to link Bloser with the ambulance-jackings."

Joe nodded. "A note saying 'I did it' would be nice. I don't know where you'd hide anything in this place, though." He wandered into the kitchen and opened a cupboard. It was bare except for two boxes of cereal. "Why do you think this Bloser guy lives in such a dive?"

Frank shrugged. He was checking the dresser drawers. "At least it's pretty clean. Look, here's the manual we used for our emergency training course." He held up a thick book titled *Brady Emergency Care.*

"Hey. That at least proves Bloser is interested in what the EMTs are doing," Joe said as he headed for a closed door. "Must be a closet." He reached for the doorknob.

"Watch that one of the stolen bodies doesn't fall on top of you," Frank said seriously.

Joe's hand froze in midair. Then he saw the corners of Frank's mouth turn up. "Sure," he said as he grasped the knob and jerked the door open.

It took Joe's eyes a second to adjust to the dim

closet. Then he gestured for Frank to come over. "I think we just hit the jackpot."

"What?" Frank stepped beside him. Joe pulled a penlight from his back pocket and shone it onto the closet walls so the two brothers could inspect them.

The walls were plastered with newspaper clippings and photos. When Joe stepped closer to read some of the articles, he quickly realized they were all about accidents in which the River Heights Rescue Squad had been involved.

"Wow," Frank gasped. "This is incredible."

"Hey—get a load of this!" Joe aimed the beam at the back floor of the closet. A scanner stood on a low box. Joe crouched next to it and flipped it on. Immediately he heard the squawk of "traffic" coming from the River Heights Rescue Squad. Joe swung around to look at Frank. "This guy's been monitoring the squad!"

Excited, he jumped up. "Bloser's been listening to calls going to and from the rescue squad. That means he knows their every move. What do you bet he's using the information to follow the EMTs on their night calls? He knows whenever there's going to be a priority four—a dead person. Then he follows the ambulance and steals the body!"

Frank looked skeptical. "It makes sense, Joe. Except that Bloser could just be a squad fanatic."

"Then we'll have to find hard proof to link him to the ambulance-jackings," Joe stated. Raising the penlight, he ran the beam over the newspaper clippings. "There!" He pointed to a clipping taped by the door. "There's our proof. That's an article on Sam Cavallo's accident!"

"And here's an article on James Squire's accident. He's the first person whose body was stolen. Still—" Frank shook his head. "It doesn't link Bloser to the ambulance-jackings."

"Okay, but it might be enough evidence to convince McGinnis to request a search warrant."

Frank raised one brow. "Based on proof we discovered when we *broke* into this place? Come on, Joe, you know the police can't do that. But they could put a tail on—"

A shuffling sound by the front door made Frank stop in midsentence.

"Somebody's coming!" Joe hissed. Grabbing Frank's wrist, he jerked him into the closet just as the front door swung open.

Chapter Thirteen

JOE HELD HIS BREATH. The closet door was open a crack. Frank stood rigid behind him, trying not to move. They heard the door shut.

Someone walked across the wooden floor and threw keys on the plastic table. Joe heard the scrape of a chair leg on the floor, then the rustle of paper.

He rolled his eyes. If it was Bloser, it sounded as though he was settling in for a while. They could be trapped there forever—or discovered any second.

Suddenly the scanner behind them let out a loud squawk. Joe jumped. He'd forgotten to turn it off!

Oh, great. Joe racked his brain, trying to think

what they could tell Bloser if he came into the closet to turn it off. They were from the health department checking for roaches?

Joe caught Frank's attention. In the dim light he could see Frank's grim expression.

But then Joe realized that the same garbled talking was coming from outside the closet. Freddie must carry a walkie-talkie or portable scanner to monitor calls no matter where he was.

"Rescue Five, assistance requested at One-one-five Bluebird Lane," the voice said over the scanner. "Male has fallen off a ladder. Possible concussion."

When the message was over, Joe strained to listen. Would Freddie leave to answer the call?

The loud scrape of the chair leg told Joe that Bloser was getting up. Seconds later he heard the door slam.

Joe and Frank stood quietly for a few minutes to make sure Bloser wasn't coming back. Joe thought about flipping off the scanner but decided that might look suspicious, too.

Finally, Frank let out his breath in a heavy sigh. "Wow, that was close, little brother."

"You're telling me." Joe pushed open the closet door and took several deep breaths. His eyes instantly darted to a newspaper on the tabletop.

"I wonder what Mr. Bloser was reading," Joe said as he and Frank crossed the room. The headlines on the front page were circled with red ink.

"Our guy's definitely interested in something," Frank stated from behind Joe.

"Yeah. And I know what it is, too— 'Reporter's Death Still a Mystery,'" Joe read aloud. "Pam Harter!" He glanced up at Frank.

His brother frowned. "Why would Bloser be interested in Pam's death?"

Joe shook his head. "I don't know. But I do know one thing—it's time to call McGinnis."

"Let's hope the Hardys have discovered something, too," Nancy said to Ned. They hovered over the sink, peeling cooked shrimp, preparing an early dinner. Already Nancy had boiled eggs and chopped onions and celery for a shrimp salad.

"Phew. I'm glad shrimp taste good because they sure are a pain to peel," Ned said. "But then I guess this must be *Frank's* favorite meal, right?"

Nancy pretended to look surprised. "Oh? I thought this was *your* favorite."

"Sure." Ned nudged her with his elbow. "You know I'm a steak kind of guy."

"That's right," Nancy teased. "I guess I got my two boyfriends mixed up."

Ned threw a shrimp at Nancy. She dodged, and it fell on the floor.

"Hey! Anybody here?" Frank's voice rang from the front hall.

"Kitchen!" Nancy hollered back.

Frank and Joe came into the kitchen, taking off their jackets as they walked. Both draped them over a chair.

"Food fight!" Joe exclaimed when he saw the shrimp on the floor.

"What did you find out?" Nancy asked eagerly. She threw the shrimp in the trash can, rinsed her hands, then turned to face the two Hardys. Ned said a brief hello, then went back to peeling shrimp.

"Lots," Frank said, grabbing two sodas from the refrigerator. He tossed one to Joe. The two sipped their drinks while they took turns telling Nancy and Ned about Renee, the stolen wallet, the traffic accident, Mike Hosford, and their visit to Freddie Bloser's apartment.

"Whew. You guys were busy. And most of it happened while everyone else was asleep," Nancy commented. Even Ned had turned around to listen.

"Yeah. So if we nod off during dinner, you'll know why," Joe said.

"You won't. Ned and I are making shrimp salad."

Frank's brows lifted. "My favorite!"

"That's what I thought," Ned muttered.

"How about you?" Frank asked Nancy. "Did you and Brenda find out anything?"

Nancy thrust a bag of croissants and a cookie sheet into his hands. "Here, put these in the oven while I tell you about Big-Mouth Brenda and her subtle interviewing technique."

An hour later the group was sitting around the kitchen table finishing up shrimp, croissants, green beans, and fruit salad.

"Man, I'm almost glad it's Hannah's day off," Frank said. "You and Ned are great cooks."

"Wait until you taste dessert." Nancy's eyes twinkled.

"Gee, I wonder what it is," Ned said. "Frank, what's your favorite?"

"Chocolate cake."

Ned nodded at Nancy. "Then I guess that's what we're having."

Nancy cocked her head. "Oh really, Mr. Know-It-All? I thought we were having lemon meringue pie—*your* favorite."

"Oh," Ned said, giving her a sheepish grin.

"So what do you think, guys?" Nancy turned back to the Hardys. "Do you think this Freddie Bloser is your body snatcher?"

Frank shrugged. "Who knows. Chief McGinnis agreed to put a tail on him. That's a start. But I'm curious about Margaret Cavallo. Why do you think Pam's investigation of her never went anywhere?"

Ned stood up abruptly. "Because it was a dead end. I told you three before that Ms. Cavallo is clean. There's no way she'd ever be involved in anything as weird as a body snatching." With those words he picked up a stack of dirty dishes and stomped to the sink.

"I think we know who he voted for," Joe said behind his hand.

Nancy shook her head. "The whole Cavallo thing has me stumped, too. And what do you think about this R.H. Diagnostics place?"

"Could be Pam was having some kind of treatment," Frank guessed. "What did McGinnis say?"

"He said the detectives on Pam's case interviewed the two technicians who work there. They didn't find anything suspicious." Nancy stood up. "Let me show you the brochure."

Her shoulder bag was on the kitchen counter. When she passed Ned, who was busily rinsing plates, she stood on tiptoes and kissed his cheek. It was kind of touching to see him so jealous, she decided.

"The clinic specializes in something called magnetic resonance imaging," she told the Hardys as she fished through her bag. "Hey, what's this?" She pulled out a lipstick tube. It was pink and said Merry Berry Red on the bottom. "This isn't mine."

Puzzled, she pulled off the top. Immediately, she realized what it was. After putting a finger to her lips to warn the others, Nancy dashed over to the counter and opened a drawer. When she found a piece of paper and pencil, she wrote out, "It's a bug. Someone's listening to our conversation!"

Frank's mouth dropped open when he read Nancy's note. She tossed him the lipstick. He inspected it, quickly recognizing the tiny, wireless microphone tucked inside the tube. Surprised, he glanced up at Joe and Nancy. Who? he mouthed silently.

Nancy shrugged. "Um, would everyone like dessert?" she asked cheerfully.

"I don't think we'll have time," Frank said. Slowly he stood up and went over to Nancy. "The person must be outside," he whispered. "You and Ned take the back door. Joe and I will take the front."

Nancy nodded, and grabbing Ned's elbow, she steered him toward the sliding glass doors that led to the backyard.

Frank gestured for Joe to follow him down the hall. If they could catch the culprit bugging them, it might just help them solve the case!

"So, Joe, do you think we'll have any exciting calls tonight at the squad?" Frank asked his brother when he opened the front door and stepped onto the Drews' porch.

"Nah," Joe said, going along with the charade. "We're due for a quiet night."

Frank stopped on the porch and listened. A faint rustling came from the bushes to his left. Slowly he went down the two steps to the corner of the house. He saw a scrap of navy blue material behind the leaves. Frank waved for Joe to go around to the far side of the bush.

The leaves rustled again. "Got you!" Frank shouted as he dove into the bushes. Grabbing the blue material, he hauled the person out backward.

"Let me go, you jerk!" a voice screeched. Spitting and clawing like a cat, the person wheeled on him.

Frank stumbled backward in surprise.

It was Brenda!

Chapter Fourteen

BRENDA CARLTON? What are you doing hiding in the bushes?" Frank asked, immediately letting go of the jacket hem he was clutching.

She jerked away, her eyes stormy. "Um, I lost a contact and—"

Joe chuckled from the other side of the bush. "Likely story. I think you were spying on us!"

Brenda crossed her arms and fumed. "Why would I want to do that?"

"Brenda!" Nancy exclaimed as she and Ned hurried around the corner of the house. "It was *you.*"

"Me?" Brenda touched her chest. "I don't know what you're talking about," she said innocently. "I was just coming over to see you,

Nancy, when these two *emergency medical technicians* whom you *don't* know very well tackled me."

"Uh-huh, then what's this?" Frank stuck his hand in the pocket of Brenda's jacket. She squealed and slapped at his arm, but it was too late.

He held up the handheld receiver, which had an antenna sticking up. "Case closed."

Nancy put her hands on her hips. "Brenda Carlton, you've done some sneaky things before but this tops them all. Where did you get that bug?"

Ignoring Nancy, Brenda bent over and brushed the leaves off her jeans. The knees of her pants were muddy.

When she straightened, Frank, Ned, Nancy, and Joe were still glaring at her. "Well, I—" she stammered. "I got it from one of the reporters at the *Times.* He's used it before to get information. I borrowed it when I knew we were going to Margaret Cavallo's office. Only she kicked us out in such a hurry, I didn't have time to plant it."

"Brenda!" Nancy protested. "You can get in big trouble for using a bugging device." She narrowed her eyes. "And when did you stick it in my bag?"

Brenda grinned smugly. "When we were in the car. You made me mad when you told me you were going to drop me off. Pretty clever, huh?"

"But why were you bugging us?" Ned asked.

"Because I knew Nancy was keeping something from me." Brenda directed her gaze at Joe, then Frank. "You did know the Hardys from somewhere else, Nancy. I was right. They're working undercover for Chief McGinnis on that body-snatching stuff. And now that I know, you'd better let me in on everything or I'll blow their cover."

Frank raised one brow. He'd been right when he'd first met Brenda—she *was* going to be a pain.

"So what do you think, Nancy," he said. "Brenda couldn't have heard that much. The tiny microphone in that lipstick isn't powerful enough to pick up much. Should we let her in on what's going on? Or tie her up and gag her until we solve the case?"

Brenda's mouth dropped open.

Nancy crossed her arms. "There's no way you can trust someone who spies on her *friends*. We'd better tie her up and gag her. We can hide her under my bed."

Brenda looked horrified. "You can't do that."

"Oh, yeah?" Frank countered. "Nancy, do you have any rope in your garage?"

"Wait!" Brenda grabbed Nancy's arm. "I promise I won't say a thing until the Hardys give me the word. That's fair. I mean, someone has to write the article when they crack their case. If they ever crack it," she added, smirking.

"Nancy, get the rope," Frank growled. He'd had enough of Brenda.

"Just kidding!" Brenda exclaimed. "I mean, I

really do want to help solve both cases. And I think I really can help—wait until you hear what I discovered about R.H. Diagnostics."

"What?" Joe asked.

Brenda crossed her arms. "Oh, no. I'm not telling until you Hardys let me in on *everything.*"

Frank rolled his eyes, then glanced over at Joe. "What do you think?"

Joe shrugged. "We'll have to tell McGinnis she knows about us."

"Okay." Frank gave Brenda a warning look. "But you'd better not blow our cover. This is serious police business, and someone could get hurt if you shoot off your mouth at the wrong time."

Brenda nodded. "I understand."

"So what's this important information about R.H. Diagnostics?" Nancy asked.

Brenda placed a finger against her cheek. "Gee, when I was listening in, I thought I heard somebody mention lemon meringue pie."

Nancy groaned. "All right, come on in and have a piece."

Frank checked his watch. "Joe and I are going to have to eat fast. Our shift starts in half an hour."

The group went into the Drews' house and Nancy quickly served everyone pie. When they were seated around the table, Brenda told them what she'd discovered.

"I read through the *Times* microfiche and

found all the past articles that had anything to do with R.H. Diagnostics."

Frank stopped chewing. Maybe Brenda would be a help, after all—at least to Nancy. "What did you discover?"

Brenda set down her fork and leaned across the table. "There were two articles about medical clinics practicing ping-ponging, and R.H. was implicated in both of them!"

"Hey, I read about ping-ponging in one of my business texts," Ned said. "That's where clinics pay each other a fee for referrals."

Joe frowned. "I don't get it."

"Say you go to R.H. Diagnostics for an X ray," Ned explained. "The orthopedist tells you you need physical therapy and recommends another clinic in the area. If you go to that clinic, the clinic will pay R.H. Diagnostics a referral fee."

"And that's illegal?" Frank asked as he polished off the last of his pie.

"Yes," Brenda said. "And I'll bet that's what Pam was investigating."

"Maybe," Nancy said. "But it doesn't sound like someone would kill her because of it."

Frank pushed back his chair and stood up. "I agree with Nancy. And now we have to go."

"Leaving us with the dishes, of course," Ned joked.

"But don't you think we should investigate R.H. Diagnostics further?" Jumping up, Brenda put her hand on Frank's arm.

"I guess."

She widened her eyes and smiled coyly. Frank looked skeptical. With a girl like Brenda that could only mean one thing—she wanted something.

Joe chuckled as he threw Frank his jacket. "Ready, bro?"

"Hey, I've got a great idea! Let me come with you two," Brenda said to Frank. "You know, ride with you on a rescue squad call. Maybe I can help you find that body snatcher."

"Uh, no, Brenda. You have to get an okay from Captain Graham to do that."

Brenda grinned. "Oh, that's no problem. My dad's a good friend of Graham."

Frank shot Nancy a look that said, Help! She just laughed.

"Maybe another time," he said quickly. "Now we've got to run. Thanks again for dinner, guys."

With a wave, he slung his jacket over his shoulder and followed Joe out the front door.

"Whew, that was a close one," Frank said when they were outside.

Joe laughed. "Which part? Brenda putting the moves on you, spying on us, or asking to ride with us on a call?"

"All three." Frank shook his head as he reached the car. "She's something, and I have a feeling that tonight won't be the last we see of Brenda Carlton. Now let's hurry and get to the squad. We need to question Luke and Jessica about Mike and Renee."

"Especially Renee," Joe said. "Maybe Luke or Jessica can shed some light on why she was messing with my wallet."

When they reached the rescue squad, there was a surprise waiting for them. Luke, Jessica, Renee, and Mike were all sitting around the lounge. When Frank and Joe walked in, Renee dropped the magazine she was reading and jumped up.

"There you are," she said, her tone accusing. "Luke—ask Joe and Frank what's going on."

"What's going on?" Frank repeated, puzzled.

A thousand questions raced through his mind. What had Renee and Mike discovered? Did they know Joe and Frank were really working undercover?

Mike Hosford stood up next to Renee, his expression grim. He was so tall, he made Renee look tiny. And his muscular arms, thick neck, and bulging thighs strained the fabric of his pants and T-shirt. Weight lifter, Frank decided. Definitely not a person you'd want to get angry.

Luke cleared his throat as if unsure how to start. "Frank, Joe—Renee found out something that concerns all of us."

Frank glanced at Joe who stood beside him, a wary expression on his face.

Renee pushed past Luke. Her dark eyes were fiery as she walked up to Joe. "I'll tell you what I found out." She locked her gaze with his, then reached around his back and plucked his wallet from his pocket.

"Hey!" Joe protested. He grabbed for it, but

Renee hopped out of reach. Flipping it open, she flashed Joe's driver's license.

"Look for yourselves," she told Luke and Jessica. "He's only seventeen!"

Furious, she spun around and threw the wallet at Joe. "And since you have to be eighteen to be an EMT, I want to know why you're on the squad, Joe Hardy, and why you stole the night job from me!"

Chapter Fifteen

"WHO GAVE YOU the right to steal my wallet, Ms. Torres?" Joe picked up the wallet, then glared down at Renee.

Tossing her sleek, black hair behind her shoulders, she glared right back. "I wasn't going through your locker to find your wallet," Renee said. "I was just mad because you guys took our jobs. I was hunting for proof that you completed your training. Your wallet was open, and I saw your birth date on your license. And I'm glad I did!"

Joe leaned closer. "Except it was none of your business."

"Now it is," Renee said, defiantly.

"Uh, excuse us, you two, but I think we need to find out what's going on," Luke interrupted.

"Right." Mike Hosford pushed past Renee and stood in front of Joe. "What're you up to, Hardy? It was bad enough that Graham booted Renee and me off our paid night squad jobs. But now Renee tells me that one of you isn't even eighteen."

"Uh, I can explain that," Joe heard Frank say smoothly.

Good, Joe thought, because I can't. They'd never discussed with Captain Graham what they should do if their cover was blown. But then they'd never figured on Renee Torres.

Joe studied her a second. She stood beside Mike Hosford, one hip thrust out as she frowned suspiciously at Frank and Joe. If she were telling the truth—that she'd only snooped because she was angry about losing her job—then maybe it cleared her of being involved in the body snatchings.

"You see, Captain Graham was worried about, uh, certain aspects of the squad, so he hired us to spy on you," Frank said. "I know we lied to you, but Graham had his reasons. I'm really a medical technician from another county he brought in to sort of go undercover. My brother has first responder training. He came along to help."

Luke, Jessica, Renee, and Mike stared skeptically at Frank.

"So what 'aspects' is Graham concerned about?" Mike asked.

"It has to do with money," Joe said, playing along with his brother's story. He waved his hand. "Very complicated. Graham's been getting flack from the county government about where funds are going. Frank's a business student who specializes in, uh, creative accounting—you know, he can tell if someone's been faking the account books."

"Why didn't Graham ask *us* if we knew anything?" Jessica asked.

"Because he suspected someone of stealing some of the private donations that support the rescue squad," Frank said. "He didn't know who to trust."

Luke and Jessica shot each other disgusted looks. "That's great to know he doesn't trust us," Luke said.

Renee and Mike looked slightly relieved.

"What about our jobs?" Renee asked.

Joe grinned at her. "You'll get them back as soon as we're gone."

"Soon, I hope," she said emphatically, then she flushed. "I didn't mean I want you gone soon—but I do want my job back. Look, I'm sorry about taking your wallet. I was a little crazy over the whole thing."

"Apology accepted."

"Hey, who wants a soda—my treat?" Renee asked, digging into her jeans pocket.

"Me," Joe said promptly. To his relief, the others declined—which meant he could escort Renee alone to the soft-drink machine. He still had some questions for Ms. Hothead Torres.

"Frank's a business student, huh," Renee commented as they walked down the hall to the squad kitchen. "And you two are undercover. Sounds intriguing."

Joe shrugged. "Nah. And since you found us out, it means we didn't do such a good job with our cover."

She looked up at him. "Yes, you have. You and Frank did a great job the night of the accident. That's one reason why I was so mad. With you two on the squad, I figured Graham would never give us our jobs back. Even when he realized we had nothing to do with those ambulance-jackings."

"You're good, too, Renee," Joe said. "Really good. I watched how professional you were that night. Even though you did leave." He gave her a questioning look.

"Everything was under control," she explained. "Mike heard about the accident on his pager. When he got there, he told me I shouldn't be helping out—for free." She handed Frank a soda.

Mike again, Joe thought. He wondered how much influence the big guy had over Renee.

When Joe turned back the way they had come, Renee stopped him with a hand in his arm. "Hey, how about going somewhere private—where we can talk?"

Joe's eyes lit up. Alone with Renee Torres sounded like a dream come true. And not only because he wanted to ask her questions. "Sounds good to me."

Ten minutes later they were sitting side by side on the stretcher in the back of the ambulance.

"Pretty romantic, huh," Renee teased.

Joe laughed. "This will be the first 'date' I've ever had in an ambulance. How about you?"

He gazed down at her. She was leaning back against the side of the ambulance, sipping her soda. "Me, too," she said. "So don't tell Luke. He'd kill us."

"I wonder if that's what the intruder was doing in the back of the ambulance the other night," Joe said offhandedly.

Renee sat up straight. "You caught someone back here?" she asked, sounding surprised. But when Joe studied her face, she glanced away.

"Yeah." Joe nodded. "At first I thought he might have tampered with something."

"Oh." Renee flushed and bit her lip. "You thought it was a guy?" she asked hesitantly.

Putting his finger under her chin, Joe tilted her face toward his. "You know who it is, don't you?"

Eyes downcast, she nodded. "Yes. It was Mike."

"That's what I thought. The person was big and obviously didn't have any trouble getting into the garage. So what was he doing?"

Renee pulled away from Joe. Drawing her legs up, she wrapped her arms around them. "You have to understand Mike. This night crew job is his life. When he was switched to unpaid day duty, he was crushed."

"Gee, sounds like somebody else we know," Joe teased.

She smiled but didn't look up. "He thought maybe he'd mess things up in the ambulances—make it look like you guys didn't know what you were doing. Only, when he almost got caught, he realized what a stupid idea it was. He didn't want to get kicked off the squad permanently."

"Umm." Joe took another sip of his drink. "At least that's one mystery solved."

Renee glanced sharply at him. "One mystery? There's another?"

"Yeah. Those missing bodies." Joe watched her out of the corner of this eye.

"Oh, that." Renee shivered. "I've been trying to block those two nights out of my head. They were so horrible. I still have nightmares."

Joe tried to read Renee's reaction. She'd looked so guilty when he first mentioned the intruder in the ambulance. Judging from her reaction this time, she really didn't know much about the ambulance-jackings. But he could always be wrong.

"What exactly did happen?" Joe asked.

"The first time, a woman came up to the ambulance at a stoplight. She was waving her arms as if she'd had an accident. When Mike opened the window, she grabbed him and put something white over his mouth. I screamed the same instant some guy jerked my door open and slapped a cloth over my face. When I took a breath, I knew it was chloroform."

"What did the two look like?" Joe asked.

"Ordinary. The police made us look through a thousand mug books, and we couldn't identify them."

"They could have been from out of town," Joe said.

"Maybe. A police car found the ambulance. Mike and I were tied up in back, still out cold. The body we were transporting was gone."

"The same thing happened both times?"

"Almost. The second time, we were en route to the hospital with the body in the back. Since the guy was dead, we weren't in a big hurry. We got an emergency call over the radio about a car accident a block away. When we pulled up, we didn't see anyone—just a van parked off the road. Mike and I both got out, and *wham,* two people pounced on us. This time they wore ski masks."

"Whew. Really weird."

"You're telling me."

Renee stretched out her legs and leaned back against the side of the ambulance. Joe leaned back, too, and slipped his arm around her shoulders. With a sigh, she dropped her head against his chest.

"The nights when the bodies were stolen—was First There Freddie at the accident scenes?" Joe asked.

"Umm. I think so," Renee said. "Why?"

Joe shrugged nonchalantly. "Oh, he was just

hanging around the other night, and Luke commented on how peculiar he was." And just maybe it adds to the proof that he's in on the ambulance-jackings, he thought.

"So how did Sam Cavallo crash?" Joe asked.

"You sure are full of questions," Renee said.

Joe shrugged again. "Oh, just curious. I'd never heard of body snatching before."

"It was a one-car accident. Mr. Cavallo had been out late, probably drinking, the road was wet, and the car skidded into a telephone pole."

"Drinking?" Joe arched one brow. "I don't remember anyone mentioning that."

"We're not allowed to give out information to the public or press about the accidents. Besides, the day after the accident, one of Ms. Cavallo's staff members called the day crew leader with a big donation."

Joe was surprised. "Isn't that bribery?"

"No. Donations keep the squad operating. I did wonder, though, why Sam's drinking wasn't in the newspapers. We even found a bottle of liquor in the car."

Joe frowned. Maybe Brenda might come in handy after all. She could check why the *Times* hadn't mentioned that Sam had been drinking.

Renee snuggled closer to Joe. "Hey, why don't we talk about something else," she suggested.

"Like what?" He looked down at her. Her long, dark hair fell like a curtain around her face, and her long lashes shaded her big eyes.

"Like why doesn't a good-looking guy like you have a girlfriend?" she teased.

"Maybe I do," he teased right back. Then bending closer, he kissed Renee's soft lips.

Umm, this is nice, Joe thought as Renee reached behind his neck and pulled him closer. The feeling that he shouldn't trust her completely flitted through his mind, but only briefly.

Kissing Renee Torres was too much fun!

"Okay, Nan, Pam has got to have more information in her computer files," Brenda said as she pawed through a container of disks. The two girls were in the office at Pam's apartment. It was morning. Once again Mr. Zeleski had let them in.

The computer was on. Nancy looked over Brenda's shoulder. "How about something on Blaine Young?" she asked. "Aren't you the overeager reporter who was going to write an article that said he killed Pam because she had information that his company was cutting corners?" Her tone was slightly taunting. "Funny that I don't remember anything about it in the news."

Brenda flushed. "All right. So I made some of it up. That doesn't mean Blaine isn't guilty."

Nancy rolled her eyes. "Well, it will be a miracle if we find anything on these disks. The police took all the disks they thought had to do with her murder. And according to Chief McGinnis, none of them held any incriminating information."

"Ah-ha! They didn't take this one labeled Christmas Present List." Brenda triumphantly held up a disk. "Let's try it."

Nancy arched one brow. "Christmas list?"

"I told you she had a weird system," Brenda said as she slipped the disk into the computer and typed in "Christmas."

When several paragraphs flashed on the monitor, Nancy pulled a chair next to Brenda's and started to read. She and Brenda gasped at the same time.

"This looks like a rough draft of an article Pam was writing," Brenda exclaimed. "And it mentions R.H. Diagnostics again!"

"Right, and it sounds like the clinic is practicing more than ping-ponging," Nancy said as she continued reading. "It's also involved in insurance fraud. Looks like Pam discovered they were sending out false and inflated claims."

"Wow. I wonder how she found that out?"

Nancy pointed to several sentences at the bottom of the page. "These must be some of Pam's notes. 'Talked to F.M. today. She passed me copies of claims.' Maybe this F.M. was her contact."

"Do you think it's someone like the receptionist?" Brenda turned to look at Nancy.

Nancy shook her head. "I don't know. And who's this? *Arthur Trusko.* Pam has his name listed at the end but nothing after it."

Just then Nancy heard a creaking noise over the hum of the computer. Instantly alert, she put her finger to her lips to warn Brenda to keep quiet. Slowly she stood up. The noise seemed to have come from down the hall.

Had someone entered the apartment?

"What?" Brenda mouthed, her eyes wide with fright. Nancy gestured for her to stay seated. All she needed was for Brenda to do something stupid.

Moving soundlessly, Nancy went to the door and peered into the hallway. She heard muffled footsteps, as if someone was walking around the apartment.

But who? And how did the intruder get in?

Nancy hunted for a weapon. Her gaze settled on a paperweight. It would have to do.

She reached for it, then after warning Brenda once again to stay put, Nancy crept into the hall. Cautiously she sneaked toward the living room. Whoever was in the apartment wasn't trying to keep quiet, as if he or she didn't realize anyone else was there.

Halfway down the hall, a floorboard creaked under Nancy's foot. She paused and held her breath. The noise from the other room stopped. The person had heard her!

Clutching the paperweight tightly, Nancy rushed into the living room. A figure wearing a ski mask and dressed in black was slipping through the closed curtains and out the sliding glass door.

"Stop!" Nancy hollered. She raced across the

carpet and pushed through the curtains covering the door. As she stepped onto the narrow balcony, someone grabbed her arm and flung her hard toward the railing.

Nancy screamed. She was going to fly off the balcony!

Chapter Sixteen

NANCY'S STOMACH slammed against the railing. She grabbed the top. Hands pushing on her back tried to force her over.

"Brenda!" Her scream split the air as her fingers slipped.

"Nancy!" Brenda screamed.

The hands released Nancy. Coughing and gasping, Nancy lay draped over the rail, trying to catch her breath. Weakly she raised her head in time to see the attacker below her. The person had jumped to the second-floor balcony, then dropped to the ground. Nancy saw the black-clothed figure disappear around the corner of the building.

"Nancy!" Brenda rushed through the open

glass doors. Grasping Nancy's shoulders, she slowly drew her back onto the balcony. Nancy doubled over. The wind was knocked out of her.

"What in the world happened?" Brenda asked.

Nancy shook her head, unable to talk. "Call McGinnis," she finally gasped. "Tell him someone broke into Pam's apartment."

"Was it Cavallo's goons? Or Blaine? I'll bet it was that jerk, Blaine, or some creep he hired!" Brenda said fiercely.

Nancy waved for Brenda to go and call. Brenda hurried into the kitchen. Still breathing raggedly, Nancy staggered back to Pam's office. She sat heavily on the chair and reached for a computer disk labeled Valentine Parties. Somewhere Pam had incriminating information on whoever killed her, Nancy was certain. That was what the intruder was searching for. But Nancy was determined to find it first.

"Boy, this surveillance stuff sure is boring," Frank muttered to Joe. The two Hardys had parked their car across the street from Freddie Bloser's apartment building. They figured he was inside since his truck was parked out front.

"Don't you think it's boring?" Frank asked, his gaze trained on the front door of Bloser's place. When he didn't get an answer, he glanced over at Joe. His brother was slumped in the passenger seat, his head resting on the back of the car seat and his mouth wide open as he snored softly.

Frank chuckled. He guessed that meant Joe found tailing Bloser boring, too. Frank yawned, wishing he could take a quick nap as well. They'd only got a couple of hours sleep the night before at the squad. It had rained all night, and a few accidents had kept them busy.

Frank thought about the case. It was going nowhere, he decided. The police tail on Bloser had turned up nothing. The guy had worked all night pumping gas, and then came back to his apartment.

After his conversation with Renee, Joe had turned up some interesting information on Margaret Cavallo. But for some reason McGinnis was reluctant to release all the information on Sam Cavallo's accident.

This morning Joe and Frank had got a look at the police report. It said nothing about finding liquor in the car. That lack of information had tipped Frank off that the department was withholding something. Plus, when he'd asked McGinnis about the accident, the chief said it wasn't important to the Hardy's case.

But McGinnis was wrong. If Margaret Cavallo was trying to hide that fact from the public, what else might she be hiding?

With a sigh, Frank looked outside. The sky was heavy with rain clouds, and a strong wind whipped the awnings and treetops.

"Rescue Five!" The 911 dispatcher's voice suddenly blasted through the car. Frank jumped and grabbed for the walkie-talkie sitting next to him. Joe's eyes snapped open. Blinking sleepily, he sat up to listen.

"Possible drownings in Muskoka River. Location at bottom of the Jefferson Bridge off Beech Street. Two males whose canoe capsized. All available rescue personnel are requested on the scene."

"Must be a bad one," Frank said, starting the car.

"What about Freddie Bloser?" Joe asked.

Frank was already pulling away from the curb. "We'll call McGinnis and see if he can get somebody over here. Besides, Freddie doesn't seem to be going anywhere this morning."

Frank steered the car deftly through traffic. The wind had picked up and leaves pelted the windshield. The bridge was only a few minutes away. When they arrived, Frank pulled off the road behind a fire truck and a police car. Ambulance No. 51 had already arrived.

Joe and Frank climbed over the guardrail, then slid down the muddy embankment to a wooded area where the rescue crews were milling about. Frank caught sight of Mike Hosford and Renee. Both wore their waterproof squad jackets.

"There!" Joe hollered. He stood on the edge of the riverbank, pointing to the middle of the fast-flowing river. All Frank could see was the head and an arm of one teenager. The boy hung on to the bow of an overturned canoe, which had been caught on uprooted trees and debris that had washed down the swollen river.

Frank shook his head. Why had two kids been canoeing in conditions like this?

Just then Mike and Renee came up.

"Where's the other guy?" Frank asked, yelling over the calls of the other people, the squawk of the radios, and the howl of the wind.

"We got him ashore," Mike told the Hardys. He gestured toward a wet-haired boy huddled under blankets. Several people in waterproof raincoats were tending to him. "He was smart enough to grab a life vest—which they both should have been wearing—and managed to swim to a branch about ten feet from shore. We formed a human chain and pulled him to safety."

"How are they going to rescue the second one?" Joe asked.

Renee pointed skyward. A helicopter was flying over the bridge and hovered over the water. But Frank could tell it wasn't going to be much help. When it tried to fly low enough, the winds threatened to blow the helicopter into the bridge.

"The police have also called in a rescue boat," Renee explained. "But we're afraid it may be too late. The kid we rescued, Jack, said his friend, Barney, the guy holding on to the canoe, isn't a strong swimmer. We've been watching him through binoculars, and it looks like he may be succumbing to cold and shock."

"And the canoe looks like it could split from the debris any minute," Frank observed.

"I think our only chance is sending someone out to get him," Mike said. "The question is, who's the strongest swimmer?"

"I am," Frank said without hesitating. "I'll go. I'll need a life vest and rope harness."

Mike nodded as if it were settled. "The fire truck crew even has a wet suit." He took off to get the equipment.

"Are you sure, Frank?" Joe asked. "You and I both took those lifesaving courses. I could do it, too."

"Yeah, but I had all that experience at the ocean last summer where the undertow was so strong," Frank said. He kicked off his sneakers and peeled off his socks. "This is similar."

Mike hurried over and handed him the wet suit. Frank took off his jacket and slid it on. It would keep him fairly warm, but still, he knew the water would be ice cold this time of the year.

On the edge of the river, the firefighters began to assemble the harness. A rope was attached to it. The men and women on shore would hold on to the rope. The trick was knowing how far upstream Frank should go so when he swam out, the current would sweep him down to the teen.

After a short debate with Joe and the firefighters, Frank walked upstream about a hundred feet. Joe came with him. Five people held the other end of the rope, playing it out slowly as Frank slid down the steep bank. When his feet hit the icy water, it sent a jolt through his whole body.

"Good luck," Joe called. He sounded worried.

"Thanks, little brother." Gritting his teeth, Frank lowered himself into the coffee-colored water. Leaves and small branches swirled in miniature whirlpools. The muddy bottom sucked at his bare feet.

Frank tried to walk as far as he could, but the swift current quickly knocked him over. With strong strokes he began to swim toward the canoe. Head up, he kept his gaze directed on his target. Barney was hidden behind the debris.

Ten feet from the canoe, Frank caught sight of him. The teen's eyes were closed, his knuckles white as he held tightly to the canoe.

Now that he was in the middle of the river, Frank could feel the current pushing him, forcing him downstream. Each stroke took more effort. Frank's breaths came in gasps.

Then the canoe shifted. Barney's eyes were wide with panic.

"Hold on!" Frank yelled. "I'm here!"

Shouts from the shore caused Frank to look behind him. Joe was frantically pointing to the rope. It had snagged on a branch floating downstream.

Wildly Frank looked around. If he swam back to untangle the rope, he might not have enough energy to swim back to the canoe.

Frank turned at the sound of a loud moan. Barney's fingers were slipping as his grasp weakened.

Frank panicked. His limbs and brain were growing numb from the cold, and he was exhausted from fighting the current. Think! he told himself.

Then Joe's voice bellowed frantically through a megaphone. "Frank! Swim toward shore," his brother screamed. "There's a log coming downstream—and it's headed right at you!"

Chapter Seventeen

FRANK SPUN AROUND in the current. He could just make out a brown object rolling swiftly on the rippling waves. Frantically he tried to swim toward shore, but the current swept him downstream, and the rope, still caught on the branch, drew taut. The log was still coming toward him.

Frank's breathing came in painful gasps. Any minute the log would be on top of him! Out of the corner of his eye, he saw someone dive from shore into the muddy water.

"Someone's swimming out to untangle the rope!" Joe hollered through the bullhorn. "When he does, we'll pull you back toward shore! But keep trying to swim this way!"

Frank gave a powerful kick just as the rope was pulled free. He shot only a few feet sideways, but it was far enough. The log sailed past, missing his head by inches.

Frank gasped with relief. His arms shook and his teeth chattered. About fifteen feet ahead of him, he could see Barney still clinging to the canoe. The log had missed him, too.

Frank was exhausted. But he also knew he was Barney's only chance. He was much closer than the swimmer who had untangled the rope. Only fifteen feet, he told himself.

Using his last ounce of energy, Frank paddled and kicked to the canoe. He slipped his arms around Barney's chest seconds before the teen grew limp. He held on to the boy while the crew on shore pulled them slowly to the bank. Strong arms grasped them both and pulled them from the rushing water.

They'd made it.

A cheer went up, then the rescue personnel went to work. Frank lost sight of Barney as Renee and Mike whisked him away. Joe and a burly firefighter hustled Frank up the bank, sat him on a tarp, and started to peel off his wet suit.

Frank tried to push them away—he didn't need to be undressed like a baby—but then he realized he was shivering so hard that his arms were shaking out of control.

When Frank's wet suit and shirt were off, Joe wrapped him in an insulating blanket, and the firefighter pressed heat packs against Frank's chest and sides. Someone brought over a hot, steaming drink.

"You okay, Frank?" Joe asked, kneeling next to him. "Or should we take you to the hospital?"

Frank shook his head. The shaking was already subsiding, and his skin was tingling with warmth.

"No," Frank replied. "You got me before I developed hypothermia. But what about Barney?"

Joe glanced up the bank toward the road. The ambulance siren rang out as Unit No. 51 took off. "I think he was in such bad shape that Renee and Mike took him to the hospital." He nodded toward a kid talking with a police officer. "That's Jack. He wants to thank you for saving his friend."

"Yeah, and I want to thank that guy who dove in and unsnagged my rope," Frank said. He glanced around. "He made it back to shore, right?"

"Yeah. With a little help." Joe stood up. "Let me see if I can find him. Then we need to get you back to Nancy's for some warm clothes."

When Joe left, Frank sipped the drink, his mind reeling. When he'd volunteered to help Chief McGinnis, he'd never thought a water rescue would be part of the deal.

"Frank?" Joe said from above him.

Frank looked up. A tall guy stood next to Joe, a blanket wrapped around his skinny shoulders. His longish hair hung in wet strings around his face. Frank thought he looked vaguely familiar.

"Frank," Joe continued, gesturing to the guy. "This is your rescuer, Freddie Bloser."

"Freddie?" Frank blurted out, but then he caught himself. Smiling, he held out his hand. Freddie bent and shook it heartily.

"Thank you," Frank said. "If it hadn't been for you, I might not have dodged that log."

"Oh, it was nothing," Bloser said, blushing. "All my life, I've wanted to work on a rescue squad."

Joe didn't know what to make of Freddie's statement. After all, this was the guy they'd been tailing. "So why don't you?" Joe asked. "All the squads need volunteers."

Freddie dropped his gaze and blushed even redder. "Because I, uh, keep failing the test even for the first responder certification. I'm not real good at memorizing stuff." He shrugged, obviously embarrassed. "But I've got a scanner so I can follow you EMTs on all your calls. And I know how you do everything—CPR, stabilizing fractures, applying antishock garments." He went on to list about ten things only someone who'd studied hard would know about. "And I've clipped and saved every article that has to do with the squad. I even took a part-time job so I could spend most of my time answering calls—just as if I were an EMT."

"Wow." Frank wasn't sure what to say. Half an hour earlier, Freddie Bloser was a prime suspect in the body snatching. Now Frank's intuition told him the guy was exactly who he said he was—someone obsessed with being on a rescue squad.

"Sounds to me like you need to keep studying," Frank said, standing up on slightly numb legs. "Maybe you could volunteer at the squad. During the day, we always need people to run the dispatch center."

Freddie's eyes lit up. "Could I go on calls with you, too?"

"You'll have to get your first responder certification first. But after you do, the sky's the limit."

"Great!" Freddie exclaimed. Grabbing Frank's hand, then Joe's, he pumped enthusiastically. "I'll see you first thing tomorrow morning."

When he left, Joe steered Frank toward the bank that led to the road. "We'd better warn the day crew we're unleashing the guy on them."

"Oh, I think he's got what it takes to make a good first responder. Someone's just going to have to help him study for the test. So what do you think about our 'suspect'?"

Joe shrugged. "I think if we or the police had dug up one shred of evidence to link him to the body snatchings, I'd want to keep my eye on Freddie. But no one has connected him in any way. And he just explained every suspicious thing in his apartment."

Frank hung on to Joe's arm as they climbed the hill. Feeling had returned to his numb feet, and his shaking had stopped, but his legs were still wobbly.

"I agree. So what's next?" Joe asked. "We've decided Renee and Mike aren't involved—"

"No, *you* decided they weren't involved,"

Frank pointed out. "After one romantic evening with Ms. Torres," he added jokingly. "I still think an EMT is in the best position to stage an ambulance-jacking. Renee and Mike might just want to get back on the night squad so they can continue helping whoever's behind the ambulance-jackings. Of all the EMTs, they're the most suspicious."

"Well, I think you're wrong," Joe said. "If we could only figure out *why* the bodies are being stolen, then we might find out *who* is doing it. Maybe we need to follow up on Margaret Cavallo," he suggested. "So far, she's the only one who might have a motive for stealing her half brother's body."

Frank snorted. "Finding out anything about her is like breaking into Fort Knox."

"Then we'll have to break into Fort Knox."

"Hey!" Frank stopped in front of the car. "That gives me an idea!"

"You want to steal some gold?" Joe asked.

"No! Better. We need to help someone steal bodies."

"Huh? Are you sure you didn't bang your head on that log?"

"Sure I'm sure. Now let's get back to Nancy's. Maybe Hannah will fix us a late lunch. We've got a plan to hatch!"

"This is the dumbest idea you've come up with yet," Ned said as he struggled to lift three huge books of wallpaper samples from the trunk of his car.

"Dumb? And here I thought it was brilliant," Nancy teased. Her arms were loaded down with rings of fabric and carpet samples.

Ned chuckled. "Me posing as an interior decorator is brilliant? I don't know one thing about the 'ambiance of living space' or whatever they say."

Nancy laughed as Ned shut the trunk. They were parked in front of Margaret Cavallo's house. "That sounded pretty good to me. And since we were able to borrow these from my friend Debbie at Superior Interiors, I'd say we look like the real thing."

"You should have got Brenda to do this," Ned insisted.

"No way. Not after she blew it the other day." Nancy shifted the sample books and turned to look at Ned. "Besides, she's busy trying to track down the mysterious F.M., the person who gave Pam that information about R.H. Diagnostics."

"I thought McGinnis was looking into that."

"He is, but his detectives are overworked trying to trace every lead. So far, they've cleared Blaine, though Brenda is still convinced he's guilty."

"How'd they clear him?" Ned asked.

"They did a voice match on the two calls on Pam's answering machine. The first call telling Pam to come to the job site in River Heights was definitely not Blaine. Plus, a parking lot attendant at Winters remembers Blaine arriving at eight-fifteen. And you know Friday evening traffic in Chicago. The police figure there's no way he could have killed Pam at seven and made it to Winters by eight-fifteen."

Nancy sighed. "Believe me, Ned," she said, and dropped her voice to a whisper, "I know that fibbing my way into the state representative's house is risky and desperate. But boy, am I feeling desperate."

Even the lead on Arthur Trusko, the name Pam had written on her disk, had gone nowhere, Nancy thought. When she'd called her father, he reported that Trusko was a respected surgeon connected with several big hospitals.

Nancy started quickly up the brick sidewalk before Ned could chicken out. When she reached the porch, she pressed the doorbell. An elderly woman wearing a black uniform answered the door. "Yes?"

"Hello!" Nancy flashed her perkiest smile and handed the woman a card that read N & N Decorators. "I hope we're not late. Ms. Cavallo said she wanted us in and out before three."

The woman frowned. "In and out?" Nancy noticed that she spoke with a strong accent.

"Yes." Nancy bustled past the woman and began looking around at the hall wallpaper and chandelier. Margaret Cavallo's house was tastefully decorated with muted colors and gleaming antiques.

"Ah, what a pleasure it is to work with someone with such impeccable taste!" Nancy exclaimed. Spinning, she smiled at the woman. Ned stood in the doorway, looking confused. The woman's brow was wrinkled with worry lines.

"Please, you have an appointment?" she asked.

"Of course!" Nancy pretended to be totally surprised by the question. "Didn't Margaret tell you? She wanted her office done by the time she finished her meeting at the county office."

"Done? You hang wallpaper that quickly?"

"Oh, yes," Ned said in a deep voice.

Nancy stepped in front of Ned. "Oh, no, Mrs.—"

"Mrs. Ju Lee." The woman bowed slightly.

"We will only be finished choosing samples to suggest to Margaret," Nancy told her. "Carpet, wallpaper, upholstery."

The woman raised one finger. "I call and check."

"That's fine," Nancy assured her. "In the meantime, we'll get started."

Nancy marched purposefully down the hall and turned left—right into the office. "Lucky guess," she muttered to Ned, who tagged right behind her.

"Are you crazy?" he hissed when she shut the office door. "I mean, I know you checked and made sure Ms. Cavallo was in a closed meeting this afternoon, but what if the housekeeper gets through to her?"

"Then we get out—fast," Nancy whispered back. But she didn't have time to argue. She needed to figure out where Ms. Cavallo kept her personal files.

"Check her desk," Nancy suggested.

Shaking his head, Ned sat down on the desk chair. Nancy placed a book of fabric samples in his lap. "In case Mrs. Lee comes in."

Carrying an open wallpaper book on her arm, Nancy slowly walked around the office. The walls were paneled, the carpet dark gold. Really ugly, Nancy thought. The office definitely needed redoing—or did Margaret like the paneling for some reason?

Reaching out with her free hand, Nancy felt along the paneling until she came to a spot where two pieces met.

"Not much in her desk except bills and government pamphlets," Ned said. "What are we looking for, anyway?"

"Anything suspicious."

"Oh well, that should be easy," Ned joked.

Nancy's gaze traveled along the wall, hunting for a break in the panel. It wasn't long before she found it, partially hidden behind a bookcase. It almost looked like a small door had been cut into the wood.

"Ned, help me move this bookcase," Nancy said.

Together, the two swung out one end of the bookcase. Crouching, Nancy pressed her fingers against the smaller panel. With a snap, it opened inward so it wouldn't leave telltale marks in the rug.

"Wow," Ned said. He stood over her. "A hiding place. Maybe Ms. Cavallo does have some secrets."

Reaching in, Nancy groped around. She felt several papers, then she touched a flat, square object. Quickly Nancy drew it out. It was a computer disk.

"Ned, look." Nancy gasped when she turned it over. "This disk is labeled Halloween. And that's Pam Harter's writing!"

Chapter Eighteen

"DO YOU THINK Ms. Cavallo had someone steal the disk from Pam's office the night Brenda was attacked at the *Times?*" Ned asked.

Nancy shook her head. "I wish I—"

Just then Nancy heard soft footsteps coming down the hall. She stuck the disk in her pocket, pushed shut the small door, then jumped up and repositioned the bookcase.

"What do you think, Nan?" Ned asked as he held up a swatch of neon green fabric against the back of Ms. Cavallo's desk chair.

Nancy grimaced.

Mrs. Lee opened the door. "I have contacted Ms. Cavallo's aide. He says you are to wait in the foyer until—"

"Oh, that won't be necessary," Nancy chirped. "Once we got in here we realized we didn't bring the right sample books. Margaret's office needs the Elegance Line, don't you think, Neddie?"

"Oh, definitely," Ned said.

Nancy gathered up all the books. "Tell Margaret we'll call her as soon as we get another break in our busy, busy schedule," she told Mrs. Lee as she swept past her and out the office door.

When she and Ned were finally outside, Nancy blew out her breath in relief. "That was close."

"Close? I'd say we got caught. Let's hope Mrs. Lee doesn't get my license plate number and sic the police on us."

"We can't worry about that now," Nancy said. "We've got the disk. I'll bet it has the proof we've been looking for."

"Let's hope so," Ned said as he slid behind the wheel. "Where to?"

"The *Times.* We'll get Brenda to run this on her computer."

"Sounds good. But let's stop on the way and grab something to eat," Ned said. "I think much better on a full stomach."

Half an hour later, Nancy and Ned hurried through the bustling newspaper office. They found Brenda in her cubicle talking on the phone. Her pencil eraser had been chewed off, and angry-looking doodles filled a blank sheet of paper.

Nancy pulled the disk from her pocket and

waved it in Brenda's face. The reporter's mouth fell open, and she slammed down the phone receiver without even saying goodbye.

"What is that?" Brenda asked, grabbing for the disk.

"Not yet," Nancy teased as she pulled it from Brenda's reach. "You tell us what you found out about F.M."

"Nothing," Brenda replied. "That receptionist at R.H. Diagnostics is so stupid she can't even remember her own name much less the names of anyone who worked there. She thinks there was a Fran somebody who sent out bills, but she left two weeks ago for a better job."

Nancy snapped her fingers. "Fran—that could be the 'F' in F.M. You're sure the receptionist couldn't remember a last name?"

Brenda shook her head. "Okay. Now, where'd you get the disk?"

"Uh." Nancy glanced at Ned. They'd already decided it was better that no one knew they'd taken it from Ms. Cavallo's house. "We'd better not tell—at least until we find out what's on it." She handed the disk to Brenda.

The reporter gasped. "That's Pam's writing."

"Correct. Now turn your computer on and let's see what's on here," Nancy said.

"Excuse me, but I'll take that," a deep voice said behind Nancy. Nancy and Ned spun around. Frazier Carlton stood in the doorway.

"T-take what?" Brenda stammered, trying to hide the disk under her paper.

Mr. Carlton frowned. Stepping past Ned and Nancy, he plucked the disk off the desk. "This," he said sharply. He glanced at it, then frowned. "Now, if you three will come to my office, I think we have some things to discuss."

"But, Daddy," Brenda whined.

"Now!" Standing back, Carlton jerked his thumb toward the door.

Brenda's mouth snapped shut. Nancy and Ned looked at each other. Nancy had no idea what Frazier Carlton wanted.

"What's going on?" Brenda whispered as they followed her father down the hall. "I've never seen Dad so serious."

"I was just going to ask you the same question," Nancy whispered back.

"I'll tell you one thing," Ned added. "From the look on your father's face, he's not taking us to a surprise party."

The disk still clutched in his hand, Mr. Carlton ushered the three into his office. When Nancy stepped inside, she stopped short. Margaret Cavallo sat primly on a sofa against the wall, her hands folded serenely, but her gaze was steely.

Crossing the office, Mr. Carlton sat behind his desk. "I believe you owe Ms. Cavallo an explanation," he said, his tone stern. "When she called Mrs. Lee and heard your descriptions, she knew right away that you were the same nosy 'reporter' who tried to interview her the other day. So she called me." He held up the disk. Ms. Cavallo's expression changed to one of shocked surprise.

"Where did you get this?" Mr. Carlton demanded.

"Uh." Nancy swallowed hard. She had to think fast. Obviously, Margaret Cavallo knew she and Ned had fibbed their way into her house. When she saw the disk, she also must have realized that they'd broken into her hiding place.

"We owe *her* an explanation?" Brenda exclaimed. "No, I think she owes *us* an explanation. Like, what is she doing with Pam Harter's computer disk?"

"I gave it to her," Mr. Carlton said.

"You?" Brenda exclaimed, sounding as surprised as Nancy felt. "But why? That's obstructing justice or whatever they call it."

Mr. Carlton sighed. "You've been watching too much TV, Brenda. Before Pam was killed, she came in to discuss certain things she'd discovered about Ms. Cavallo's family. She knew I'd supported Ms. Cavallo's campaign, and she wasn't sure what she should do with the material. I told her I felt it was personal and should either be destroyed or given to Ms. Cavallo. I felt that nothing would be gained by printing it."

"Even if it meant Pam's murderer might get away?" Nancy asked.

Ms. Cavallo turned cool eyes to her. "Ms. Drew. I know your father. He is a wonderful man. He also talks highly of you and your detective skills. That's why when Frazier told me who you were, I knew it was time we talked. But what we discuss remains confidential. Do you understand?"

Mr. Carlton wagged a finger at Brenda. "That means no scoops," he warned.

Brenda nodded meekly.

"My half brother died in a car accident. He was drunk. The only information on Pam Harter's disk is about my half brother and his alcoholism, which killed him. But now he is dead. It is bad enough his body has disappeared. I don't want his memory tarnished, too."

Or don't you want his memory to tarnish your career, Nancy wondered. "Is that why the police have also suppressed evidence?" she asked.

"The police have grilled me thoroughly, Ms. Drew," Ms. Cavallo continued calmly. "I have held back nothing. But Chief McGinnis is also a friend and supporter. He knows how much the information about my half brother would hurt my family."

Nancy shifted. She was trying to read Margaret Cavallo. Was the representative sincere? Or was this all an act? One thing was certain—she had lots of powerful allies in River Heights.

"Ms. Cavallo, I want to apologize," Nancy said sincerely. "I realize now that you couldn't have been involved in any crimes."

"What?" Brenda protested. "Nancy, have you flipped?"

"No, Brenda. All Ms. Cavallo's trying to do is protect her family. If your father gave her Pam's disk, there was no need for her to kill Pam or break into her apartment to get it."

And there was no need for her to snatch Sam Cavallo's body, either, Nancy thought, since the rescue squad, police force, and the press were already keeping any scandalous information from the public.

Nancy wasn't sure that was ethical, but it certainly took away any motive Margaret Cavallo might have had.

Ms. Cavallo bowed her head slightly. "Thank you for the apology, Ms. Drew. I hope you find Pam Harter's murderer."

After Nancy, Ned, and Brenda left Frazier Carlton's office, Brenda turned to Nancy. "Well, thanks to you, there goes our best suspect," she grumbled.

"Not really." Nancy tapped her chin in thought as they walked down the hall. "Since whoever broke into Pam's apartment wasn't after that Halloween disk, that leaves at least one disk we found with incriminating information."

Ned snapped his fingers. "The stuff on R.H. Diagnostics!"

"Right. Hand me your phone, Brenda." Nancy said when they reached her cubicle. "I'm calling Chief McGinnis to find out if they've discovered anything interesting about the clinic. Then I'm making an appointment tonight at R.H. Diagnostics!"

* * *

Sitting in the waiting room of R.H. Diagnostics, Nancy filled in the information sheet. One other person was in the room, an older woman who flipped through a pamphlet and yawned. Then a young girl came out of the office, and the woman rose to leave with her.

Earlier Nancy had tried to get the receptionist to talk. But Brenda was right. The most intelligent thing Miss Suki Simpson had done in the past fifteen minutes was file her nails and call out, "Next."

But then Miss Simpson may not have been hired for her brains, Nancy thought. Maybe she'd been hired because the last girl who had worked in the office had been too smart. Had Frank figured out all the illegal things that R.H. Diagnostics was up to? Had she then gone to Pam? Was that why Pam had made an appointment? To find out what was going on at the clinic?

So many questions, Nancy thought. Especially since the police had found out that Pam hadn't kept her Friday afternoon appointment. And that Miss Fran Milstein, the mysterious F.M., still hadn't been found.

Nancy stood up and paced across the stuffy room. Ned and Brenda were stationed outside in Ned's car. Nancy hoped they didn't get nervous and come rushing in before she had even seen the technicians. Grabbing up the clipboard with her filled-in information sheet, Nancy stuck it through the slot in the glass. Now Suki was putting on bright red polish.

"Um, Miss Simpson, may I use the bathroom?" Nancy asked.

"Down the hall, third door to the left," Suki said without missing a stroke.

"Thank you." Nancy pushed through a closed door. The hall shone bright with fluorescent lights and recently waxed tile. Slowly she walked to the bathroom, peering through open doorways. She saw X-ray equipment in one room and a strange machine in another. One door was shut. When she paused to listen, she heard murmurs of conversation.

Nancy blew out a breath in frustration. The place looked like a regular doctor's office. But then it should have. The clinic was performing medical services. It was the billing and record-keeping that were bogus.

Nancy was dying to take a look at the files. Since there were no file cabinets in the cubicle with Miss Simpson, she figured they must be stored elsewhere.

Turning left, Nancy went into the bathroom and washed her hands noisily. When she came out, she peered down the hall.

The place was quiet. The door across the hall was shut. Nancy scurried over and cracked open the door. Bingo—two desks and a wall of file cabinets.

Slipping inside, Nancy carefully shut the door. This is crazy, a voice inside her said. Someone's going to catch you. But she had to find proof that R.H. Diagnostics was so involved in illegal practices that Pam might have been killed in order to hush up her discovery.

Nancy opened the top drawer of the nearest file cabinet. The files inside were color coded, the patients' names on the outside tabs. Quickly Nancy searched for Harter, Pam. Nothing.

She opened the second drawer. It was packed with folders and forms. Nancy realized that going through the clinic's files would take forever. She had to figure out a way to break in later.

A noise outside the closed door made Nancy freeze. Slowly she slid shut the drawer.

Suddenly the door swung open, and a stocky woman in a white lab coat stepped in. "Excuse me, but why are you in here?" she demanded. The name S. Criswell was written over the pocket. She had short, brown hair and piercing blue eyes.

"I'm really sorry," Nancy said. "But the receptionist told me the bathroom was the third door on the right. I walked in and shut the door before I realized this wasn't the right room." She smiled sheepishly. "I'm Nancy Drew, your seven-thirty appointment."

Ms. Criswell glanced down at a new file folder she was holding. "Yes, Ms. Drew. Follow me, please. So Dr. Jones referred you to us?"

"Correct." Nancy nodded as she followed the woman out the door and down the hall. She'd used her family doctor's name. Still, her palms were sweaty and her heart raced. Had Ms. Criswell bought her story?

Stepping aside, Ms. Criswell showed Nancy into the X-ray room. "What seems to be the problem?"

"I've been having a pain in my wrist," Nancy said. "Dr. Jones wanted it x-rayed to rule out a hairline fracture."

"Um." The technician grunted while she wrote on a piece of paper.

Nancy's heart started to slow down. So far, so good, she thought.

"Then I guess we'd better x-ray it," Ms. Criswell said. She dropped the folder on a table, turned, and shut the door. Then she leaned against it, her blue eyes turning icy cold.

"So, Ms. Drew, did you really think I was that stupid?"

"Uh, I'm not sure what you're talking about," Nancy said, trying to sound calm.

"Oh, yes, you do." Criswell took a step closer, a nasty smile distorting her lips. "I heard the clunk of that file drawer closing."

"I backed into it by mistake," Nancy explained.

"Oh, really?" Criswell arched one brow. "Then how do you explain the fact that Dr. Jones, a doctor who has never referred one patient to this clinic, suddenly happened to refer you."

Good question, Nancy thought. She swallowed hard. "I suggested you. A friend used your clinic and was very satisfied."

Criswell laughed. "A friend, huh. You mean a fellow reporter—Pam Harter?"

Nancy shook her head vehemently. "I've never heard of Pam Harter."

"Really? I'm surprised. She was in all the papers." Criswell grinned. Reaching up, she pulled a syringe and a needle from her breast pocket.

Nancy's eyes widened. The syringe was filled with a liquid.

"You see, she was murdered," Criswell said coolly. Nancy watched in mounting horror as the lab technician stuck the needle onto the end of the syringe. "Because she was nosy, too. So Ronald and I got rid of her. Just like we're going to get rid of *you!*"

Chapter Nineteen

NANCY STOOD FROZEN, her gaze riveted to the syringe in the lab technician's hand.

The crazy woman was going to kill her!

The realization shocked Nancy out of her trance. She ducked behind the X-ray table. She glanced right, then left, searching for a way out. She knew the woman had locked the door into the main hall. But to Nancy's right, there was another door that probably led into another examining room.

Criswell made a clucking sound and shook her head. "No way out. And the receptionist and other patients are gone, so don't bother screaming."

Holding up the syringe, she squirted out a tiny drop of liquid. "But don't worry, you won't feel anything but the prick of the needle. Not like poor Harter. We had to strangle her so it would look like her boyfriend did it."

"You're insane," Nancy said, trying to stall. If only Ned and Brenda would get nervous and come rushing in! "I really don't know Pam Harter. I just came in for an X ray!"

"Gee, your wrist looks all right to me." Criswell glanced down. Nancy was clutching the edge of the X-ray table so hard her knuckles were white. "Let's see, what was Harter complaining about? Chest pains? Luckily, we'd been tipped off by our lovely ex-employee, Fran. So when Harter came in, we knew she wasn't here for medical services. Though I must say, Fran was reluctant to tell us that information."

"You killed Fran?" Nancy's voice came out in a hoarse whisper.

Criswell raised one brow. "Oh, so now you're willing to admit you were snooping? Not that I ever believed your story. Especially since I saw you the day I broke into Harter's apartment. Too bad I didn't knock you off the balcony. And too bad I didn't permanently knock out that other nosy reporter in her office!"

The blood rushed from Nancy's face. "Okay, I'm not here for an X ray. But I'm not a reporter, either. I'm a private detective. And my partners know I'm in here. If I don't come out soon, they'll break into the place looking for me."

Criswell hesitated a second. Then she cocked her head. "Well, they won't find you."

"Maybe not right away, but—"

Criswell started to laugh. "No, I mean *they won't find you.* When the boss gets through with you, there won't be anything left to identify."

"The boss?"

"Trusko. Believe me, he's not going to let some punk kid interfere with a million-dollar-a-year business."

Trusko! Nancy's mind raced. So Pam *had* written Arthur Trusko's name for a reason. The respected surgeon was behind all this. But how? And why?

"Now quit stalling. Harter tried to talk her way out of it when she realized we weren't meeting her with information about R.H. Diagnostics. And look where it got her—murdered."

"You met Harter at the building site?"

"That's right. Pretty clever, huh? We lured her there with a bogus message from her boyfriend. When she saw us, she got a little nervous. But then we told her we had a big scoop for her. You should have seen her eyes light up. She let me get right in the car. Stupid lady." Criswell chuckled crazily. Then her face turned stony. "And now it's your turn."

She lunged around the table toward Nancy. Nancy dodged around the other end and raced for the door to her right. She could hear a noise on the other side. Brenda and Ned!

"In here!" Nancy yelled the same time she grabbed the doorknob. She yanked open the door—and ran smack into a giant of a man in a lab coat! He caught her by the shoulders.

"Going somewhere, Miss Drew?" he asked.

Nancy shuddered. The guy was huge with a bushy mustache and yellow teeth. The name R. Wentz was written over his coat pocket.

After jerking back her leg, Nancy kicked him in the shin. He screamed in pain. When he reached down to grab his leg, she started to push past him, but he grabbed her hair and yanked her to a halt. Then Wentz locked one arm around her throat and drew her back against his chest.

"Hold the witch still," Criswell growled. "She's more trouble than Harter." Raising the syringe, the technician stepped toward Nancy.

Nancy cried out, hoping Ned and Brenda was close enough to hear. But Wentz's arm choked back the sound, and all that came out was a strangled gasp.

Nancy's eyes widened as Criswell's leering face drew closer. Then the needle plunged into her arm, her head started to spin, and Nancy knew she'd lost the battle.

"Well, Joe. Do you think plan B is going to work?" Frank asked his brother as he drove the ambulance down a dark, tree-lined street.

Joe shook his head. "I hope so. We're out of suspects. If this doesn't ferret out our body snatchers, then I don't know what we'll do. You nervous?" He glanced over at Frank.

"Yeah." He pulled up at a stop sign and glanced over his shoulder. He could see Rescue Ralph, the dummy, lying on the wheeled stretcher, tucked and strapped in just as if he were a real patient. "Both Graham and McGinnis agree that this is the only way. You ready to make that call?"

Joe nodded, then picked up the microphone to the radio. "Let's just hope our body snatchers are monitoring our calls tonight."

"And that they're eager for a fresh body," Frank said grimly.

"Rescue Five calling River Heights Hospital," Joe said into the microphone.

"Go ahead, Rescue Five."

"This is EMT, Joe Hardy. We're transporting a fifty-year-old male patient who despite CPR and advanced life-support measures died at his home, address One-oh-five Willow Lane, at ten o'clock. We are en route to the hospital. Estimated arrival time is fifteen minutes."

"Ten-four, Rescue Five. We'll be expecting you."

With a nervous sigh, Joe replaced the microphone. "Okay. No one but Graham, McGinnis, you, and I know this is a fake call. We've got the right ingredients to lure out the body snatchers—a late-night run and a recently deceased person."

"We even gave our body snatchers an address so they can figure out what route we'll take to the hospital," Frank added as he cruised slowly down Willow Lane, the siren silent.

He and Joe looked at each other. They knew this was the only way. But they both knew how risky it was, even though McGinnis had unmarked cars tagging along—close by, Frank hoped. He glanced anxiously in the side mirror. The suburban street looked deserted.

Frank accelerated and turned down a side street that led to the highway. His fingers tensed on the steering wheel.

"Don't forget, Frank," Joe said. "Renee told us that the last time, the snatchers ambushed them. We've got to be on the lookout."

Just then a woman backed down a drive, almost running into them. Frank swerved just in time. He caught a glimpse of her face before she sped off. It was pale with fright. Next to her on the seat, a child lay with its head in her lap.

"Hey. That looks like a mother with a sick kid," Joe said, leaning forward to get a better look. "Maybe we should tail her to the hospital and make sure she gets there okay."

Frank nodded. Ahead of them, the woman's car careened from side to side. "Looks more like something's wrong with the driver to me!" Frank picked up the microphone. "I'll radio for help."

Suddenly the car shot across the street, jumped the curb, and crashed into a tree.

Frank hit the brakes. "We've got to help her!"

Quickly the two Hardys grabbed their primary

bags and jumped from the ambulance. Frank rushed to the driver's side. The woman was slumped in the seat. The child had rolled onto the floor.

Behind him, Frank heard the squeal of tires as another vehicle stopped. Joe jerked open the door of the passenger side.

"Miss, are you okay? We're EMTs," Frank said as he reached into his bag for a light so he could check out the woman's injuries.

"Hey, Frank," Joe said from the other side. "This isn't a kid, it's a—"

Frank heard a muffled gasp. Glancing up, he glimpsed Joe struggling with someone. The person's arms were around Joe's shoulders. A white cloth covered his nose and face.

"Joe!" Frank hollered at the same instant the woman bolted upright, grabbed his neck, and yanked him toward her chest. Behind him, someone put a cloth against Frank's mouth and nose. He tried not to breathe.

Flailing out with both arms, he whacked the woman in the head. Then his arms were jerked behind his back as a second person held him still. The woman held the cloth over his face.

Don't breathe, Frank told himself frantically. Desperate, he kicked out, hoping to connect with the woman, hitting instead the side of the car with his ankle. The force of the blow made tears come to his eyes. His lungs felt as if they were about to burst.

"Breathe, you punk!" the person hollered behind him.

Frank's lungs screamed for air. Finally, unable to stand it any longer, he took a huge gulp of air. Immediately his head felt light. Feigning unconsciousness, Frank let his body go limp.

"Finally," the woman said. She held the cloth over his nose for a few seconds more. Then roughly, Frank was tossed to the side of the road.

"Now let's get that body," the woman said. "Fast."

Frank strained to listen. He heard the back doors of the ambulance opening. Then he heard a cackle.

"Hey, Ace, get a load of this," the lady yelled. "There's a dummy back here."

"A dummy?"

Frank tried to concentrate on what they were saying. But his brain felt fuzzy.

"Oh, great. Wait'll Criswell hears about this," the woman said. "It's lucky we have that Drew girl. Otherwise, the boss would be furious."

"Drew girl," Frank mumbled, feeling a momentary stab of panic. Then his eyes rolled back in his head and everything went black.

Chapter Twenty

JOE COUGHED. Something was pressing down on his cheeks and the bridge of his nose. He was being chloroformed!

Jerking upright, Joe struck out with both fists. His eyes were open, but everything looked blurry.

"Hey!" someone hollered. "Cool it or we'll have to strap you down, Hardy!" Two pairs of strong hands forced him to lie back.

Joe blinked. Chief McGinnis's face swam into focus. Then he rolled his eyes upward. Jessica stared upside down at him, her freckled face concerned.

That was when Joe realized the thing pressing on his face was an oxygen mask, and he was lying on the wheeled stretcher. He tore off the mask and sat up.

"Where's Frank? Is he okay? Did you get the two body snatchers?"

McGinnis patted his shoulder. "One question at a time, Joe. Yes, Frank is okay. He got chloroformed, too. But the oxygen seems to be bringing him around. And yes, we got the body snatchers." He nodded to two handcuffed people standing among a dozen police officers.

Joe stared at the two. One was the woman who crashed the car. She was yelling shrilly at the officers about her rights. The other was a short, stocky guy wearing dirty jeans. A number of police cars blocked the road. In the middle stood Luke and Jessica's ambulance, the Hardys' ambulance, the woman's smashed car, and a white van. Strobe lights flashed and radios squawked. On the outskirts, people who lived on the block, some wearing robes and jackets over pajamas, stared curiously.

Joe saw Frank sitting on the curb, holding an oxygen mask over his nose. Luke stood next to him. Frank waved and took off his mask. Then standing on shaky legs, he came over, Luke supporting his elbow.

"Well, Hardy, we did it," Frank said when he lowered the mask.

Joe grinned. "Yeah. Us and half the River Heights police force."

Frank tried to sit down on the stretcher and almost fell. Luke and Jessica each caught an arm.

"Whoa, buddy," Luke said. "You're still really woozy."

"That's for sure," Frank lowered himself slowly, then clutched his head in his hands. "What a headache. The police came to the rescue just in time."

"An unmarked car was about two blocks behind you," McGinnis said. "Those two were about to jump into their van when the officers nabbed them."

Joe shook his head. "Boy, were we both fooled. Frank and I were so worried that a mother and her child were in distress, we didn't expect an ambush." He told Chief McGinnis how the woman had deliberately wrecked the car. "When I opened the car door to check on her kid, I immediately realized it was a dummy. But then it was too late."

"The body snatchers were clever, all right," McGinnis agreed. "They were driving stolen vehicles so we couldn't trace them." He frowned and rubbed his chin. "And their drivers' licenses say they're from out of town. That leads me to believe there's got to be a local person involved. They have to take these bodies somewhere close by."

The police chief sighed and ran his fingers through his gray hair. "And already they're demanding lawyers because they say we entrapped them. Anyway, unless they talk, it's going to take a while to find out where they took the bodies and why."

Joe groaned with frustration.

"Well, I'm just glad the EMTs are off the hook," Luke said.

"Even if you two Hardys did lie to us!" Jessica said angrily.

Joe started to explain, when he noticed how white Frank's face was. "Maybe we'd better get you back to the Drews'."

"Drew!" Frank suddenly looked up, his eyes frantic. "Where's Nancy?"

"Nancy?" McGinnis and Joe glanced at each other.

"She's probably at her house waiting to hear how plan B went," Joe said.

"Oh." The panic in Frank's eyes died, and he slumped back on the stretcher. Joe frowned. What was all that about Nancy? he wondered. Was his brother totally out of it?

"I'm taking you guys in the ambulance," Luke said. "And no arguments."

Twenty minutes later they were stretched out on lounge chairs in Nancy's family room. Even though it was almost midnight, Hannah had woken up and was fussing over them.

"More tea, Joe?" she asked, holding the steaming pot.

"No, thanks. But another one of your blueberry muffins would sure make my head feel better."

"Hannah, where's Nancy?" Frank asked. He had a cold compress on his forehead, and the color was returning to his cheeks.

"She's out with Ned."

"On a date?"

"Well, actually, she had an appointment at some medical clinic. Then she said she and Ned were having a late dinner."

"Oh." Frank grew silent. He frowned, and stared down at his teacup.

Joe knew there was definitely something wrong with Frank. "This is great, Hannah," he said. "But you know, it's getting late. Why don't you go to sleep."

Hannah suppressed a yawn. "Well, it has been a long day." After saying good night, she went upstairs.

When she was out of earshot, Joe said, "Frank, something's really bugging you. What's going on?"

"I'm not sure." Frank rubbed his temples. "But I get this anxiety attack every time I think about Nancy."

Just then someone banged loudly on the front door. Joe jumped from the lounge chair. Frank spun around to stare down the hall. "What in the world?" Joe strode down the hall.

As he neared the door, he heard urgent calls. "Joe! Frank! It's Brenda!"

Joe unlocked the door and yanked it open. From the sound of Brenda's voice, she was nearly hysterical.

"Hey, you'll wake Hannah," he cautioned as Brenda rushed into the foyer.

"I'm so glad you're here?" she cried, immediately bursting into tears.

Frank dashed down the hall.

"What's wrong?" he asked.

"It's Nancy," she sobbed.

"Nancy!" Frank exclaimed. He grabbed Brenda's arm and shook it roughly. "Pull yourself together, Brenda, and tell us what happened."

"Frank!" Joe pushed him back. "Let's take her to the kitchen. We don't need to wake Hannah and worry her to death."

Putting an arm around Brenda's shoulders, Joe led her to a chair in the kitchen. "It's okay," he said soothingly. "Now calm down and tell us about Nancy."

Between sobs, Brenda told them about Nancy's appointment with R.H. Diagnostics. "After we waited about forty-five minutes, we saw the receptionist leave. Ned went up to the office and banged on the door. There was no answer, and the lights were out!"

A fresh sob racked Brenda.

Joe looked up at Frank, who was pacing back and forth.

"What happened then?" Joe asked, handing her a tissue.

Brenda wiped her eyes. "Ned went around back to look for another entrance. All of a sudden, a van roared from the back. Ned came running from around the building, trying to chase down the van. When it got away, we went after it. As Ned drove, he told me what happened. He said that when he was coming around the corner to check for another entrance, he saw two people putting something in the van. They slammed the doors shut, but Ned swears they were putting a person in back. He caught a glimpse of reddish blond hair—he thinks it was Nancy!"

Frank groaned. "Oh no! I was right—something did happen."

"Where's Ned now? And why did it take you so long to get here?" Joe demanded.

"We tailed the van, then lost it." Brenda blew her nose. "Ned dropped me at a pay phone and told me to call McGinnis. When I couldn't get him, I called the rescue squad looking for you. Finally, I got someone who said the EMTs had just called in and they were en route to the Drews' to drop you both off. I called a cab and came over as fast as I could."

While Brenda was talking, Frank paced nervously in front of her chair. Then suddenly he started toward the hallway. "All right, enough talk, let's go find her," he said brusquely.

Joe put a hand on his arm to stop him. "But we don't have a clue where she is."

"I do!" Brenda picked up her purse by her feet and opened it. "I had the cab stop at the *Times.*" She pulled out some notes. "When the van whizzed past, I saw faint lettering. 'Medical Supplies.' I couldn't read the name, but I remembered Pam Harter had written about a medical company in one of her files."

Frank stopped pacing, and he and Joe both looked over Brenda's shoulder.

"Were these Pam's notes?" Joe asked.

Brenda shook her head. "No. The information was on a disk Nancy and I found in Pam's apartment. We wrote down anything that looked important."

Joe scanned the information. It was about R.H. Diagnostics and its insurance and ping-ponging scams.

"There's the name!" Brenda tapped on the paper. "Finest Care Medical Supplies. Nancy and I thought R.H. Diagnostics might be using them as a phony company to launder dirty money from their scams. I'll bet that's the name that was on the van."

Joe rushed over to get a telephone book to look up the address. "Let's hope that's where the van was headed," he said grimly.

"Who is this?" Frank asked. Leaning over Brenda's shoulder, he pointed to the bottom of the paper. "Arthur Trusko."

"Some big-shot doctor. Nancy couldn't find anything scandalous on him. But she must have discovered something *very* wrong at R.H." Brenda looked up at Frank. "Otherwise, why would they have kidnapped her?"

Suddenly Frank's face turned white, and he groaned. Joe stopped flipping through the phone book to stare at him.

"Oh, no, now I remember what's been bothering me. Those goons who ambushed us tonight expected a body for whatever evil scheme they were into." Frank clutched the back of Brenda's chair tight. "When the woman saw all we had was a dummy, she said, 'It's lucky we have that Drew girl. Otherwise, the boss would be furious.'"

Frank turned his frightened gaze to Brenda and Joe. "That means the body snatchers are connected with R.H. Diagnostics. And they have Nancy!"

Chapter Twenty-One

BRIGHT OVERHEAD LIGHTS made Nancy blink rapidly. She tried to raise her arm to shield her eyes, but for some reason, she couldn't move. Then she realized she was lying on her back, bound tight!

A scream welled up in Nancy's throat before she realized her mouth was taped shut. Panic seized her. What was going on? Where was she? How had she got here?

She was able to raise her head enough so she could see the length of her body. Four leather straps secured her to a metal table. The straps were so tight, they bound her arms to her sides and her legs to the table.

For a second she studied the room. It was small

and except for a bare bulb hanging overhead, dark. From the musty smell, Nancy figured it was a basement. There were two doors on opposite sides of the room. Both were shut. The walls were solid concrete with no sign of a window. Next to her was another metal table.

Exhausted, Nancy dropped her head. Criswell and Wentz must have brought her there, she decided. But why? Why hadn't they killed her?

The name *Trusko* swam into Nancy's brain. The two lab technicians had called him the boss. Maybe they were consulting with Trusko right now, deciding what to do with her. What had Criswell said—that when Trusko was done with her, no one would be able to find her?

Nancy didn't even want to think what that meant.

She racked her brain, trying to figure a way out of this mess. She didn't remember anything after the shot Criswell had injected. She didn't even know what time it was. Had Brenda and Ned figured out she was missing?

A sudden feeling of anger washed over Nancy. Criswell and Wentz may have killed Pam, but they weren't getting her, too.

Furious, she struggled, trying to pull her arms free of the straps, but they only seemed to tighten. Then she heard the sound of a door opening. Her heart began to race.

Ned poked his head into the room.

Tears filled Nancy's eyes.

"Nancy!" Fear mixed with relief flooded Ned's face as he raced over to the table. "I'm so glad I found you," he whispered as he quickly started unbuckling the strap pinning Nancy's arms.

Out of the corner of her eye, Nancy saw the door swing open wider and Wentz step in.

"Unh! Unh!" she grunted behind the tape and frantically bobbed her head, trying to signal Ned.

He whirled, but it was too late. Wentz grabbed Ned's arm and flung him against the wall. With a loud whack, Ned hit the concrete blocks and slowly slumped to the floor.

Moving rapidly, Wentz crouched on top of Ned, holding him down with a knee on his chest. The same instant, he whipped a handkerchief and bottle from his pocket.

Nancy watched with wide eyes as Wentz shook something onto the handkerchief and held it over Ned's nose. For a second, Ned came to and struggled. Then his eyelids drooped, and he became limp.

"Did you figure out who broke the window?" Nancy heard someone say. Criswell walked into the room. She'd taken off her lab coat and was wearing black pants and a sweatshirt. When she saw Ned, she stopped short.

"Who's that?" she asked Wentz.

Stuffing the handkerchief back in his pocket, Wentz stood up. "Must be the detective's partner she was talking about."

Criswell glanced at Nancy and chuckled. "So

much for your partner, lady. Strap him on the other table," she told Wentz. "Trusko will be delighted. Two bodies! Makes up for that mess tonight with the ambulance from the rescue squad."

Two bodies. Rescue squad! Nancy's stomach flip-flopped. Criswell and Wentz must be connected to the body snatchers Frank and Joe were trying to catch!

Wentz grunted as he hoisted Ned's limp body up and dumped him on the other table. "You're right—that was a mess. Do you think those dopes we hired, Sandy and Ace, are going to blab to the cops?"

Criswell nodded. "Sooner or later. That's why Trusko wants to get out of here. These two will be his last."

His last what? Nancy screamed inside. What was Trusko up to?

"So hurry up," Criswell added. "We need to get out of here, too. As soon as Trusko's finished, we're suppose to torch this place as well as R.H.—get rid of any evidence."

Wentz secured the last strap around Ned's limp body, then redid Nancy's strap. "Bound tight. Is Trusko coming?"

"Any minute," Criswell replied as the two went out the door.

For a second, Nancy squeezed her eyes shut. She remembered Joe and Frank telling her briefly about plan B. They must have caught the hired goons. But that left Wentz, Criswell, and Trusko.

"Good evening, Miss Drew," a voice said politely.

Nancy's eyes snapped open. A handsome, gray-haired man was leaning over the table, smiling down at her. "I'm Arthur Trusko, famous surgeon. I believe in reassuring my patients before I begin such a delicate operation. That way you can relax."

Operation! Nancy's eyes widened. She couldn't believe what she was hearing. Blinking her lids and grunting, Nancy tried to let Trusko know that she wanted to talk.

"What?" Trusko bent closer.

Nancy dropped her chin and jerked her eyes toward the tape over her mouth.

"Oh! You'd like to talk. Of course. But only if you don't scream," he chided. Gently Trusko peeled off the tape. Nancy inhaled deeply.

"Better?" He smiled, his expression concerned. "Those two cretins I hired don't know how to treat my patients."

Nancy pressed her lips together, not sure what to say. It was obvious the guy was nuts. "Thank you, Dr. Trusko," she began, trying to keep her voice from quavering. "I'm glad to meet such an eminent physician. But, um, I was wondering if you could tell me what you're going to do with Ned and me?"

Trusko frowned. "You mean the admissions nurse didn't explain the procedure?" He *tsk*ed. "I must remember to reprimand her."

Definitely mad, Nancy decided. But then

Trusko laughed as he plunked a leather medical bag onto the table next to Nancy's side. "Ah, I love a good joke."

He opened the bag and held up several glistening scalpels. Nancy's brows shot up. "I—I don't understand," she stammered. "Are you really going to operate on us?"

"Yes—I need your body parts," Trusko said.

"My body parts?" Nancy croaked.

"Heart, liver, kidneys, lungs, corneas," he recited as he carefully laid the scalpels on a silver tray. "Do you know that you are worth more dead than alive? Why, I can get at least twenty-five thousand dollars for a healthy heart like yours and fifty thousand dollars for one kidney. It's a very profitable business."

Nancy was so stunned, it took her several moments for the information to register. "You mean, you want my organs for transplants? Isn't that illegal?"

As well as deadly! she thought, panic rising in her chest.

"Oh, definitely—at least in this country. But fortunately, there are many other countries that aren't so backward. They have clinics and hospitals that specialize in transplants. It's a big business to them. After all, each year thousands of people die because there aren't enough kidneys for transplants. To me—that's the real crime."

"Not as much of a crime as your killing Ned and me for our organs!" Nancy exclaimed.

Trusko rolled his eyes as if he were talking to a child. "My dear, I wouldn't be killing you if you hadn't poked your nose in my business. You and that snoopy Harter reporter. Too bad I couldn't take her lovely organs." He sighed.

"But the other bodies I used were already dead," he continued. "So I wasn't hurting anyone. Well, except for our accountant, Miss Milstein." He shrugged. "That couldn't be helped. But it's all for a good cause. People overseas are *dying* for the organs I send them."

He chuckled at his joke, then began pulling on rubber gloves. "But now Criswell tells me tonight was all a setup—a dummy was planted in the ambulance. Can you imagine? And worse, the people Criswell hired to snatch bodies got caught. I guess it had to happen. Luckily, I was ready to flee the country. No one appreciates me here. So I have a flight to London out of Chicago early this morning. I've been invited to join a famous transplant unit in Southeast Asia. They'll be so excited to hear I'm bringing them two sets of healthy organs, don't you agree?"

Nancy's heart was beating so hard she couldn't answer. This is only a nightmare, she told herself wildly. I'm not really about to be carved into pieces!

Nancy tilted her chin, trying to see around Trusko. Was Ned still out of it? His lids fluttered, but his mouth was slack.

"Now, no more questions, Ms. Drew." Trusko smiled warmly. "It's time to prepare you for surgery." He reached into his bag and pulled out a needle and syringe. "Don't worry, you won't feel a thing."

"There it is!" Joe hollered from the backseat of the rental car. "Finest Care Medical Supplies."

A crooked sign with faded lettering hung beside the door of the dark warehouse. One streetlight illuminated the area that housed several other warehouses, some behind chain-link fences.

"This is the place?" Brenda questioned as Frank zipped next to the curb. She was sitting in the passenger seat. "But it looks deserted."

"It's our only lead," Frank said grimly. He opened his door and jumped out. Joe climbed out beside him.

Brenda slid over into the driver's seat, and Frank handed her the keys. "Head back to that phone booth we spotted and get the police out here," he instructed her. "Then stay at the corner to flag them down."

Brenda nodded and started the car. Joe was glad that for once she wasn't arguing.

When Brenda zoomed off, the two Hardys hurried to the front door of the building. It was locked.

"It doesn't look as if anyone's been in the place for a while," Frank said, running his finger over the dirty knob.

Frustrated, Joe smacked his fist into his palm. "There's got to be another entrance." Stepping back, he surveyed the front of the building. It was constructed of metal siding with a flat roof and no windows. "You think there's an alarm system?"

"We'll soon find out. Let's check around back." Frank broke into a jog. A drive led down to a lower level equipped with a loading ramp, dock, and two bays with garage doors.

"There's Ned's car!" Joe said. "And the van!"

They raced down the drive to the van. It had been backed up to the farthest loading bay. Ned's car was parked at an angle beside it as if he'd stopped in a hurry.

Joe jerked open the back doors of the van. The inside was empty. "Let's check the registration," he said.

"No time." Frank spun around and ran up the ramp to the right-hand garage door. "I got the license number. But right now we've got to find Nancy—before it's too late!"

Vaulting onto the dock, Joe tugged on the left-hand garage door. "Locked, too." Anxiously he peered around. "There's got to be a way in. See if you can jimmy the lock. I'm going to look around the other side."

He jumped off the dock, then took off up the drive along the side of the building, searching for a way in. Halfway up the slope, he saw a rectangular window set at ground level. The glass had been completely broken.

Joe dashed to the corner of the building. "Frank, over here!" he called in a low voice.

When Frank reached him, Joe was already lowering himself feetfirst through the window.

"It's a tight squeeze. Ned must have got in this way," Joe said. "Which means the goons may not have captured him."

"Shhh," Frank warned. "From now on we use commando tactics. It's likely there's a guard. We have surprise on our side."

Joe hung down as far as he could, then dropped. He fell about a foot before he landed on a concrete floor. Glass crunched under the soles of his tennis shoes.

When he glanced around, all he could see was blackness. As his eyes adjusted to the dark, he made out a furnace in the far corner. Next to it Joe saw a crack of light under a door. A second later Frank dropped down next to him.

The Hardys stood frozen, looking and listening. Joe pointed to the crack of light. A voice came from behind the closed door.

"You knock," Joe whispered. "When the door opens, we'll both rush in and surprise attack whoever's in there."

Then a scream rang out, echoing and bouncing through the dark room.

"That's Nancy!" Joe exclaimed.

He ran for the door, Frank right behind him. Hand outstretched, he grabbed the knob the same instant two black shapes hurtled from behind the furnace. A gloved hand chopped Joe's wrist away from the knob.

Gritting his teeth against the pain, Joe dove for

the closer black-clothed figure. Behind him, he heard Frank scuffling and then a groan. Joe's fist connected with the person's jaw, but the person retaliated by using his head to butt Joe in the stomach.

Joe landed heavily on the floor. But before he could stand up, a gunshot rang through the basement like a crack of thunder.

"Get up," a woman's voice growled as a toe booted Joe sharply in the side. "Get up before I kill you and your buddy!"

Chapter Twenty-Two

FRANK MOANED as he held the back of his aching head with one hand. Warm blood oozed between his fingers where he'd been hit with a gun butt.

It didn't matter that his head was spinning. He had to help Nancy!

When he tried to rise from where he knelt on the floor, someone kicked him sharply in the ribs.

"I told you to stay down," a woman's voice barked. Frank fell back onto the concrete floor.

"Frank, are you all right?" Joe whispered from somewhere beside him.

"Shut up," a man's voice ordered. "So, Criswell, what are we going to do with these two?"

"I don't know," the woman named Criswell snapped. "We need to ask the boss."

The boss. Was it Trusko? Frank wondered. Did he have Nancy?

Frank tilted his head, trying to see Joe. His brother's arms were held tight behind him by a guy the size of a building.

Slowly Frank rotated his head toward the woman. Her back was to the window. The dim light from outside glinted off the barrel of a revolver. It was aimed steadily at Frank's head.

"Get up," Criswell ordered.

Tensing, Frank clenched his fists. Maybe if he dove for her legs—

"And don't try anything stupid," she added, lowering the barrel so it was inches from Frank's temple. "I won't hesitate to use this, and Wentz will break your friend's neck with one snap."

"Do what she says, Frank," Joe said.

Slowly, still holding his head, Frank stood up. Rage glittered in his eyes as he glared at the woman, who held the gun on him.

Behind her, Frank saw a slight movement—a shadow dancing on the wall. He tensed. Was someone there?

"I can't believe that Drew detective had *three* partners," the woman muttered. "Maybe we can get rid of these guys when we burn down R.H. Diagnostics. Unless Trusko wants their bodies, too." She chuckled nastily.

"Wants our bodies?" Frank repeated. He hoped that the goon holding on to Joe wouldn't see the movement behind Criswell.

Out of the corner of his eye, Frank saw the

shadow raise its arm. Then he heard a crack as something connected with bone. The woman slumped forward, the gun flying from her fingers. It skittered under the furnace.

"Make that four partners," Brenda said as she stepped over the woman, an emergency-size flashlight in her hand.

Frank grinned at her, then spinning, he flew at Wentz. Taking advantage of the surprise, Joe had thrown himself backward into the big guy, smacking him against the wall. Together, the two Hardys managed to get Wentz's arms behind him and his face pressed down into the floor.

Panting, Frank looked over at the fallen woman. Brenda was tying her wrists with an electric cord. Her hair had fallen out of her ponytail, and her cheeks were smudged with dirt. Maybe Brenda wasn't so bad after all, Frank thought.

"Good work, Carlton," he whispered.

"Thanks. And don't worry, I called the police. They should be here any minute."

Frank nodded toward the man still struggling underneath him. "Help Joe tie this guy up. I've got to see about Nancy."

As soon as Brenda had Wentz's wrists secured, Frank jumped up and threw open the door by the furnace. His heart leapt into his throat. Nancy was gagged and strapped to a table, her eyes staring at him wildly. On a table beside hers, Ned was strapped down, too. His eyes were open, but he looked groggy. No one else was in the room.

"Nancy!" Frank crossed to the table. Quickly

he unbuckled the first strap. When her arms were free, Nancy reached up to tear off the tape while he unbuckled the strap around her waist.

"It was Trusko!" she gasped when the tape was off. "He's getting away. There!" Shakily she pointed toward the door opposite Ned's table.

Frank raced to the door. He flung it open and ran into a huge storage room full of boxes. There were two garage doors on a long wall. One of the doors was wide open, and Frank could see the loading area behind the building.

He raced outside just in time to hear the roar of a motor as the van zoomed up the drive.

Quickly he ran back to Nancy. Brenda was helping her release the last strap while Joe unbuckled Ned.

"Trusko got away," Frank said.

"When he heard the fighting outside, he panicked," Nancy explained. "And just in time. Ned and I were about to become organ donors."

"What?" Brenda, Joe, and Frank chorused.

"He's the one behind the body snatchings! He sold the organs from James Squire and Sam Cavallo's bodies to overseas buyers. From what he was telling me, he got huge amounts of money." Nancy swung her legs to the side of the table. Frank held her elbow as she slowly slid to the floor.

"So Trusko was the mastermind behind the ambulance-jackings," he said. "Wait until Graham and McGinnis find out!"

For a second Nancy swayed unsteadily. "Is Ned all right?" she asked.

Joe was helping Ned sit up. When she was by Ned's side, Nancy grabbed his other elbow. "Are you okay?" she asked him.

He rubbed his forehead. Wincing, he touched the back of his head. "Man, I don't know what hurts more. What happened?" He glanced from Joe to Nancy with a dazed expression.

"We'll explain later. We've got to get Trusko," Nancy said. She helped Ned slide off the table.

"But we don't know where he went," Joe said.

"Really, Nancy," Brenda chimed in. Now that she was in the light, Frank could see her pants were covered with dirt and her jacket was ripped. All her courage must have been used up knocking out the woman, because now her eyes were wide with fright. "Let's wait for the police," she pleaded.

"Can't." Cupping Ned's elbow, Nancy led him toward the door. "Trusko's headed overseas. If he leaves the country, we'll never catch him."

Frank moved to stand in front of Nancy. "That's true. We can hardly track Trusko across the ocean."

"Right, but we *can* catch him at the airport. He's headed to London, then Southeast Asia. By the time the police mobilize, he might be gone. Also, I'm not even sure the police will believe me when I tell them Trusko's a criminal, and I don't have time to convince them now. Even McGinnis will tread carefully before arresting a reputable surgeon. The police might even think the shot Criswell gave me made me imagine things."

Frank exchanged glances with Joe.

Joe shrugged. "Nancy's right. Who's going to believe some high-powered surgeon is carving up people and selling their organs? I hardly believe it myself. And I'll bet those two goons we caught in the ambulance ambush never even saw Trusko. They were probably hired by Wentz and Criswell."

"That's right," Nancy said. "Criswell and Wentz killed Pam Harter because Pam knew too much about the scams R.H. Diagnostics was into—also masterminded by Trusko. Unfortunately, Criswell was the intruder we surprised that day in Pam's apartment. She recognized me when I came into the clinic. So she gave me a shot. When I woke up, Trusko was ready to cut out my vital organs."

Ned's mouth dropped open. "They were going to kill us for our organs?" Anger flashed in his eyes, and he straightened. "My head's feeling better already. Let's go get this Trusko guy. I don't care if he is some hotshot doctor."

"But catching him still isn't going to get us the proof that he was behind it all," Brenda protested.

Nancy turned to face her. "You're right, but there's no other way. We've got to keep him from getting on that plane. Maybe you should stay here, Brenda, and wait for the police. Tell McGinnis *everything.* He just might believe our wild story."

Brenda nodded. "Okay. But I'm not waiting in here," she said, nervously glancing at the stainless-steel operating tables. Frank put his arm around her shoulder, and together they went out to the storage room.

"Will you be all right?" he asked Brenda before climbing into Ned's car.

She smiled. "Yup." Standing on tiptoes, she kissed him softly on the lips.

Frank was too surprised to kiss her back.

"I'll be fine." Brenda said. "Actually, I'd rather stay here. I'll be the first to get the story!" Her expression grew serious. "You guys get Trusko. Nancy's right. You have to catch him before he leaves the country. He's behind everything—including my friend Pam's murder!"

"Let's check the departure screens," Nancy said when they reached the concourse at the airport an hour and a half later. "Find any flights to London. Since I'm the only one who can identify Trusko, we'll have to stick together."

"There—Gate Ten," Joe pointed at the schedule. "Leaves in forty-five minutes."

"Let's check it out." Nancy led the way. Impatiently she, Ned, Frank, and Joe waited while they all cleared the security gates.

"At least we know Trusko can't get through with a gun," Ned said.

"Ready to go," Frank said. He'd been the last one through the security gate. Nancy took off down the wide aisle of the concourse. It was past midnight, so the terminal was fairly empty.

When they reached Gate Ten, Nancy surveyed the people sitting in the waiting area. Most were slumped tiredly in their seats. "No sign of him," Nancy said, frustrated.

"Could be he's waiting in the VIP lounge," Joe said. "In that case we'll just have to watch when the passengers board."

"So what's the plan when we do see him?" Ned asked.

Nancy bit her lip, not sure herself. She knew it was a hasty decision to go after Trusko. But she also knew if he made it out of the country, the River Heights Police Department might not have enough evidence to convince authorities to bring him back.

"Let's hope Brenda convinces McGinnis that we haven't lost our marbles," Nancy said. "I think we need to do anything we can to delay Trusko getting on the flight—or delay the flight itself."

Ned shook his head doubtfully. "I don't know, Nan. Sounds chancy."

Just then an announcement came over the microphone. "All passengers with small children or those who need assistance may now board Flight One-sixteen to London."

Several people in the waiting area stood up, gathered their things, and began to form a line.

Nancy stood off to one side, partially hidden by a pillar. Ned and Frank hung around nearby. Joe stationed himself near the woman collecting the boarding passes.

Suddenly Nancy tensed. Trusko was walking toward the boarding area. In one hand he held the leather medical bag. A topcoat was draped over his other arm. He strode confidently down the concourse as if he didn't have a care in the world.

"That's him," Nancy said between clenched teeth. When he drew nearer, she stepped in front of him.

Trusko stopped dead. "Miss Drew?" he stammered.

"Surprise, Trusko," she said. Immediately Ned and Frank flanked him. Arms folded, they glared at the gray-haired doctor.

Regaining his composure, Trusko smiled graciously. "What seems to be the problem?"

"The River Heights Police Department would like to ask you some questions," Nancy said, her gaze boring into his. "But don't worry. You're not under arrest. In fact, when I explain your transplant procedures, they'll be very interested."

Trusko raised one brow. "Oh, really?"

Extremely interested, Nancy thought. "Yes, it seems the medical community wants to make buying and selling organs legal," she fibbed. "Perhaps you need to stay in the United States—you know, to lead the movement." She knew this was a lame argument, but she just hoped she could keep him talking and off the plane.

"Well, that's a switch. Of course, bone marrow and tissue are already actively sold in the private market." For a second Trusko looked thoughtful, as if he was considering what Nancy had said. Then he raised his head and bellowed, "Security! Security! I want these three arrested for harassment!"

Immediately two guards jogged up. Startled, Nancy jerked her chin around. Ned and Frank whipped around to face them, too.

"These kids are hassling me, and I have a flight to catch," Trusko snapped.

"Hassling you!" Nancy retorted. Spinning, she faced the nearest guard. "He's a criminal wanted for questioning by the River Heights police."

"She's crazy." Trusko pursed his lips. With flashing eyes, he set down his medical bag and pulled his wallet from his back pocket. "I'm Dr. Arthur Trusko," he said, showing the guards his driver's license, then his passport. "These whackos are from some lunatic animal rights group, and they're keeping me from boarding."

The one guard touched Nancy's arm. "There's no soliciting allowed, miss," he warned, while the other guard stepped between Ned and Frank, taking their arms.

"She's not crazy," Ned protested as he jerked his arm from the guard's grasp. "Call the Chicago police for verification."

Trusko's eyes flashed angrily. "And have me miss my plane! I'll sue the airport for unlawful detainment. Now let me through."

He snatched back his license and passport, picked up his medical bag, and pushed his way to the front of the line. Nancy watched helplessly as he handed the boarding agent his ticket.

"Hold on!" A third guard jogged up, his walkie-talkie pressed to his ear. "We've gotten a communication from the Chicago police to hold that guy. They're on their way."

That was all Nancy needed to hear. "Stop him!" she called as she ran between the rows of chairs in the boarding area.

Trusko snapped his head around, the gleam of confidence dying in his eyes. Quick as a cat, he grabbed the boarding agent's wrist and spun her in front of him. His right arm clutched her neck tight, and his topcoat fell to the floor as his left hand pressed into the small of her back.

Nancy skidded to a stop. Ned, Frank, and two of the guards were right behind her.

"Don't move," Trusko warned, his gaze darting from Nancy to the others.

Nancy froze. The boarding agent's eyes widened with horror.

A woman behind Nancy screamed. The rest of the people in line were shocked into silence.

"In my left hand, I've got a syringe filled with a very lethal drug," Trusko told them in an icy voice.

Nancy's gaze darted to his hand. She could see the gleam of the sharp needle.

"So if you don't let me board my plane immediately," Trusko continued, "and let it take off, this woman will die a very painful death!"

Chapter Twenty-Three

"WE CAN'T LET TRUSKO get away!" Nancy said to Frank and Ned as the doctor backed down the jetway that led to the plane, dragging the terrified boarding agent with him.

Behind Nancy, walkie-talkies squawked noisily as the guards talked with the security dispatcher. Several other men and women in uniforms began ushering the people in line back to the waiting area.

Nancy whirled and grabbed the nearest guard's arm. "You can't let the plane take off!"

Frowning, the guard pulled away. "You need to stand out of the way, miss. We're handling this now."

"Nancy," Frank said softly. "We've got to let

airport security and the police take over. They're trained to deal with situations like this."

Frustrated, Nancy stared at the milling airport personnel. A voice over the walkie-talkie squawked out, "Ramp control to tower, what's the procedure? Can Flight 116 be cleared to leave the gate?"

"Jenkins to control tower," the guard said back. "Tell ramp control not to authorize anything. We're waiting for the hostage-negotiating team."

Nancy groaned. If Trusko used the attendant as a hostage, they'd have to let him go! Angrily she smacked her fist against her palm. That meant the guy who'd almost turned her into a pile of organs would end up going free!

"Where's Joe?" Nancy asked.

Frank shook his head. "He disappeared. You don't suppose—"

"—he's on the plane!" Nancy cut in excitedly. "We have a chance to get Trusko yet!"

"Nancy!" Ned put a restraining hand on her arm. "Frank's right. Let airport security handle this."

"I can't." Breaking away from Ned, Nancy raced down the jetway. When she reached the entrance into the plane, she slowed to a walk.

Joe, where are you? she wondered. If the two of them could get close to Trusko—they might just have a chance.

Peeking cautiously into the plane, Nancy

quickly realized it was a jumbo jet, a 747. Nancy glanced to the right. Several flight attendants hurried up and down the aisles, trying to settle frightened passengers. To the left, a spiral staircase led to the upper deck, which housed the flight deck and lounge.

Loud voices from above told her that Trusko had headed there. Nancy darted to the stairs and climbed quietly to the deck.

The lounge area was deserted. To her right, the door into the flight deck was half open. Nancy could see most of the boarding agent. Her cheeks were flushed, her eyes glazed with fear. Trusko had one arm circling her neck. He had the syringe pressed against her back.

"Take off!" she heard Trusko order. "Take off now or I'll kill her!"

"We're not getting clearance," someone said.

"You'd better do as he says," another voice chimed in.

Nancy recognized it instantly. It was Joe!

She crossed the lounge and ducked beside the doorway. Craning her neck, she peeked inside, trying to spot Joe. Trusko's head was turned away as he talked to the captain, who sat in front of Trusko in the left seat. Then she saw Joe, a flight attendant's smock tied over his white polo shirt. He stood opposite Trusko next to the empty flight engineer's seat behind the copilot.

"Listen to the flight attendant," Trusko was saying. "He's the only smart guy. If you take me to where I want to go, I won't hurt anyone. If you stall *one second longer,* Ms. Harliss here will die an agonizing death in front of your eyes!"

"I guess we have no choice," the captain said. "But if we're flying straight to Southeast Asia, then I insist we let the passengers off. Otherwise, the jet will be too heavy to make it all the way—we'll use too much fuel."

"That's fine. Just do it fast." Trusko chuckled, the sound macabre. "Then prepare for takeoff. I'm on my way!"

Out of the corner of his eye, Joe saw Nancy duck out of sight behind the doorway. If only she could distract Trusko, he thought, feeling desperate.

The captain had told Trusko the right thing. Even if he had no intention of taking off, the delay unloading the passengers would give security a chance to figure out how to immobilize the madman.

And Trusko was definitely mad.

Suddenly loud shrieks came from the other side of the door. "Stop the plane! Stop the plane! My daughter! She's not on board!"

"What in the—" Trusko swore. "This better not be a trick." Impatiently he turned the boarding agent toward Joe. "You, get rid of that hysterical mother," he growled the same second Nancy burst through the doorway, flinging the door open with a loud bang.

The distraction was all Joe needed. He aimed a sharp karate kick at Trusko's right leg. His foot hit Trusko's kneecap so hard, the doctor jerked backward, screaming with pain. The boarding agent pulled away and, unhurt, fell onto the back of the pilot's seat.

Joe dove on top of Trusko, grabbing for the syringe. But just as fast, the doctor pulled his left arm out of reach, then jabbed the air, aiming for Joe's head. Joe threw himself to the side, but when he glanced up, the gleaming point of the needle was plunging toward his leg.

Suddenly a hand whacked down sharply on Trusko's wrist, knocking the syringe from his grasp. Trusko screamed in frustration as Joe lunged on top of the doctor and pinned him against the flight engineer's seat.

Instantly Nancy dropped beside Joe and snatched up the syringe, while the copilot jumped from his seat and grappled with Trusko's flailing legs.

"Do you have him?" Nancy gasped.

Joe nodded. "Yes. Thanks to you."

Then above him he heard a voice say, "Captain to control tower. Situation under control. But get Security in here—fast!"

"So this is what River Heights looks like during the day." Frank gazed around appreciatively.

Nancy laughed. "You didn't get much sightseeing in while you were here, did you? I'm glad we were able to plan a picnic before you left."

Nancy and Ned were laying a checked tablecloth on a picnic table. Next to the grill, Joe and Renee were blowing and poking the coals, trying to get them glowing hot.

It was a gorgeous day. The sun shone bright on the Muskoka River, and the recent rains followed by the warm day had finally convinced the daffodils and tulips to bloom.

"Here." Nancy handed Frank a package of hot dogs. "See if our two scouts have that fire going."

Just then a car roared into the parking lot of the picnic grounds. When it screeched to a halt, Brenda climbed out, carrying a huge picnic basket.

"Who invited her?" Ned grumbled.

"I did," Frank replied.

All eyes turned to Frank.

"Hey-y-y, big brother," Joe teased as he and Renee joined the group at the table.

"I invited her, too," Nancy said quickly. "After all, she helped solve this case."

As Brenda approached, she waved gaily. She was wearing shorts and a matching shirt.

"Is this the meeting of the crime solvers?" Brenda asked as she put her basket on the table.

Frank nodded. "Yes. And I'm about to use my olfactory senses to sniff out some clues." Bending, he smelled the basket. "Fried chicken?" he asked.

She frowned. "Chocolate cake! Isn't that your favorite?" She pulled a foil-covered pan from the basket.

Everybody laughed.

"So what's the latest on Trusko and his accomplices?" Brenda asked Nancy.

"According to McGinnis—"

Brenda held up her hand. "One second." She reached into the basket and pulled out a small tape recorder. "Now go ahead," she said, pressing the record button.

"Didn't your story already make yesterday's headlines?" Ned asked.

Brenda grinned proudly. "Yes, and today's, too. I just happen to have copies hot off the press." She turned off the recorder, then reached into the basket and pulled out several copies of *Today's Times,* which she passed out.

"And here I thought there was food in there," Joe joked.

"'Teen Sleuths Solve Reporter's Murder,'" Brenda read aloud.

Nancy skimmed the article, "Gee, Brenda actually mentioned our names once—that's a first," she whispered to Ned. The two were pouring cups of lemonade for everyone.

"Yeah, but did you notice *her* name is mentioned about ten times?" he whispered back.

"Now go on with your story," Brenda said, pressing the record button again. "Daddy says tomorrow's headlines are all mine, too."

"Well, according to Chief McGinnis," Nancy began, "the big guy, Wentz—"

"The one who threw me against the wall," Ned grumbled.

"And tried to wrench my head off," Joe added.

"—is blabbing everything. It seems Criswell did most of the dirty work," Nancy continued. "She murdered Pam and the bookkeeper, Fran Milstein—"

"That's the F.M. in today's big story," Brenda cut in. "You know, there's enough material here for one of those true crime novels," she added.

"Did the police ever find Fran's body?" Joe asked.

Nancy shook her head. "It seems Fran was Trusko's second organ donor," she said, grimacing. "When he was through operating, he had Criswell cremate what was left."

"That's gross!" Renee exclaimed.

"You said it," Frank agreed. "James Squire was the first Trusko did, and Sam Cavallo the third. He shipped the organs overseas in special containers. The forensic guys are having a field day at First Care Medical Supplies, where Trusko did his operating. But it will take weeks to identify all the evidence."

Renee shuddered and leaned against Joe. "It's like some horror movie. I'm just glad the whole thing's over. Now that Mike and I are back on the night squad, I don't want any more of that body-snatching stuff."

"So what's going to happen to Trusko?" Brenda asked.

Nancy switched off the recorder. "You really need to get that from the D.A.," she said firmly.

"Okay," Brenda grumbled, putting the recorder back in the picnic basket.

"From what McGinnis told us, Trusko's going to have so many charges brought against him that he'll never get out of jail," Frank said. He began ticking them off on his fingers. "Kidnapping, attempted murder, illegally selling organs, stealing bodies, attempted hijacking of a plane—"

"That reminds me, Joe," Brenda cut in, pulling a pad from her shorts pocket. "How did you ever manage to get on that jet?"

Joe grinned. "Used the old Hardy charm."

Nancy, Ned, and Frank burst out laughing.

"Tell Brenda and Renee how you really did it," Ned said.

"Well, when I saw Nancy confront Trusko, I realized he wasn't going to go quietly. At the same time a family rushed up to the boarding agent. They must have had a dozen kids—all crying. I just got in the middle of the group." He chuckled. "I even held one of the little girls' teddy bears as we walked down the jetway. When we got into the plane, the flight attendant was so busy folding strollers and wiping tears that I sneaked in unnoticed. I saw a flight attendant's smock hanging over a seat. The rest you know."

"Pretty clever," Renee said admiringly.

Frank snorted. "You should have heard the chewing out Security gave him for doing that. I thought they were going to put handcuffs on Joe instead of Trusko!"

"Lucky for Joe, Chief McGinnis arrived with the Chicago police and vouched for him," Nancy told Brenda.

"And as for Trusko," Frank continued the story, "since they connected the 'reputable' doctor to R.H. Diagnostics, the police can add insurance fraud and ping-ponging to that list of offenses."

Joe nodded solemnly. "The guy's in big trouble."

"Yeah," Ned chimed in. "He hired some hotshot lawyer who's trying to get him off."

Nancy shook her head. "I just don't understand how a brilliant doctor could have become so depraved."

Frank wiggled his brows menacingly. "You never heard of Dr. Jekyll and Mr. Hyde?"

"Oh, I knew Trusko was guilty all along," Brenda said.

"Really?" Ned remarked, his tone innocent. "What about that article you were going to write blaming it all on Blaine Young?"

"Hey, Blaine is a jerk. Did you see in the society pages that he's dating some gorgeous model already?"

"He still wasn't a murderer," Nancy pointed out.

Brenda put her hands on her hips. "Well, you were convinced it was Margaret Cavallo," she shot back. "And you two Hardys thought it was that Freddie guy."

Joe shrugged. "Well, he *was* pretty suspicious."

"Now he's doing fine as a volunteer at the squad," Renee added.

"That reminds me." Nancy reached for her

bag and pulled out four tickets. "Ms. Cavallo sent me a nice thank-you note. She and her family were relieved to find out what happened to her half brother's body, so she sent free tickets to her next fund-raiser."

"Whoopee," Brenda said.

"I say we should go," Ned said. "Those things usually have great food."

Nancy shook her head. "I'm not going. I don't like the way our state representative used her power to hide information from the public."

"Oh, grow up, Nancy," Brenda said. "That's what all politicians do."

"Well, I know one thing," Frank said before Nancy had a chance to retort. "That chocolate cake sure smells good. When do hungry detectives get to eat?"

"Right now," Joe said, walking over to the grill. "The coals are ready. Grab a hot dog or hamburger and throw it on."

"Wait—first I propose a toast," Ned said, reaching for his lemonade. "To all of us—for solving River Heights's most gruesome case."

"Hear hear," everybody chimed in, laughing as they tapped their paper cups together.

"And to Brenda Carlton," Brenda added, her tone extra-smug. "For her Pulitzer Prize–winning headlines."

Nancy bit her lip, holding back a laugh.

"Well, at least she's back to being the old Brenda," Ned whispered in Nancy's ear.

"That's for sure." Nancy chuckled.

"We'll be leaving tonight," Frank told everyone. "Maybe next time, Nancy, you can come to our hometown and join us in a case."

"Not without me," Ned said quickly, slipping his arm around Nancy's shoulders.

"Or me," Brenda said, smiling at Frank, who almost blushed.

Ned snapped his fingers. "Hey, if the Hardys are leaving and Brenda's busy writing, and Renee's saving lives on the night crew, does that mean you and I finally get our romantic evening together?"

"Sure," Nancy said, smiling up at him. "At least until the next case comes along!"